"... confound it, woman!"

Ben's voice increased in volume as he jumped to his feet.

"I am making you a proposal of marriage."

Harriet began to feel the walls of the room close about her. She fumbled for something to say.

"Oh, but I . . . I hadn't thought about it," she admitted. "I am twenty-six, you know, and had rather put marriage out of my mind."

Something of Ben's irritable manner evaporated, and his voice lowered in a most agreeable fashion.

"See here, Harriet," he began. "It's a peculiar sort of situation for both of us. But you're a fine-looking girl and have a good brain, and I wouldn't mind, so why should you?"

Before she could answer, Ben flashed her a dazzling smile and strode from the room with all the confidence of a peacock.

You wouldn't mind, fumed Harriet. *But I daresay I would!*

Dear Reader:

Welcome! We're glad you joined us for our new line, Harlequin Regency Romance. Two titles a month, every month, for your reading pleasure.

We know Regency readers want to be entertained, charmed and transported to that special time of magic and mischief. And we know you also like variety, so we've included everything from the Regency romp to the dramatic and touching love stories that Harlequin is famous for. We offer you authors you know and love, as well as new authors to discover and delight in. We feel we have captured the Regency spirit and are proud and pleased to share it with you.

Harlequin Regency Romance was created with you, the reader, in mind, and we'd like nothing better than to know what you think. If there's something special you would like to see included, drop us a line. If there's any way we can improve, we'd like you to tell us. We welcome your feedback and promise to consider it carefully. After all, you are our biggest fan.

We hope you enjoy reading Harlequin Regency Romance as much as we enjoyed putting it all together. And, in the true tradition of the Regency period, "we wish you happy" and look forward to hearing from you.

Marmie Charndoff
Editor

THE UNEXPECTED AMERICAN

ANN HULME

Harlequin Books

TORONTO • NEW YORK • LONDON
AMSTERDAM • PARIS • SYDNEY • HAMBURG
STOCKHOLM • ATHENS • TOKYO • MILAN

Original hardcover edition published in 1988 by
Mills & Boon Limited.

Harlequin Regency Romance edition published August 1989

ISBN 0-373-31108-7

CHAPTER ONE

THE MAN PUT one hand on the surface of the wall thoughtfully, appraising it as one who contemplates scaling it. He was so tall that his head almost reached the top, and it required very little effort to pull himself up on powerful shoulder and arm muscles and take a look at the far side. He saw a coppice of trees, silent and deserted, and dropped back into the lane, dusting off his grimed palms.

It presented no problem. It was of the dry-stone variety, typical of this part of the West Country. It offered excellent toeholds, and although built entirely without mortar, was as solid as if it had been a piece of sheer rock. It was, however, a little slippery with frost. Although it neared mid-day, the winter sun had not reached through the overhanging boughs of the coppice beyond, and the stones were damp and lightly touched with silver. The man made his decision. He had travelled this far unseen, and had no wish to be observed now. He had hung about in this lane long enough. It ran along the boundary of the estate and its surface was plentifully scored with frozen cart-ruts, denoting that it was well used. Sooner or later, some farm labourer on his way home for his mid-day meal would come lumbering along, and the tall man in the lane had no wish to encounter anyone. In the country, a stranger was always an object of curiosity and question. He jumped up, grasped the top of the wall, swung his long legs over it, and dropped down lightly on to the overgrown tangle of dead nettles and greenery blackened by winter cold.

His arrival in the thicket caused little upset. A solitary robin dived away in its darting, swooping flight to settle on a nearby bough and fix him with a bright, suspicious eye. Otherwise, though he listened carefully with an ear well tuned to those slight significant sounds which herald danger, he could hear nothing, and began to make his way through the coppice. After a few moments, he found himself on the very edge of it. Facing him was a stone bridge over a small river, and beyond that lay a broad expanse of lawn which swept, rising slightly, towards a large grey stone house in the distance. This was the southern aspect of the house. The porticoed front of it faced the west, and looking in that direction he could see the small figures of a chaise and pair of the sort that was usually hired by someone wishing to make a longer than usual journey, not keeping a carriage and pair of his own. There was a visitor at the house. He had probably called on business and his visit was nearly over, for the chaise was clearly waiting for him to come out. The watcher in the trees found his eye taken by a movement at a long window in the south-facing side of the house. The slender figure of a woman passed before it and then back again with a restless movement. A frown touched the watcher's forehead. He retired a little into the coppice, and settled down to wait and watch.

HARRIET STANTON, turning up and down the room, passing and repassing the window which gave on to the lawn, clasped her hands nervously and exclaimed in a low, emotion-filled voice, "It may be legal; it most certainly is not just!"

Her companion, an elderly man whose aspect would have indicated "lawyer" even to the most casual observer, gave a sigh and stretched his legs. He had not enjoyed the journey here by hired chaise. He was over sixty years of age, and felt it. He would like to retire, and could do so comfortably. However, before he did, he had a duty to settle the Stanton estate, not least because he had known Harriet Stanton since she had been in leading-strings, and was very fond of her— fond of both girls, but of Harriet especially.

"My dear child," he said soothingly, "we must look on the bright side, be a little optimistic."

"Optimistic!" cried Harriet, whirling to face him, the grey skirts of her trim riding-habit swirling about her slender, almost boyish, figure. In an age which had abandoned hoops and tight lacing in favor of flimsy gowns and natural curves, her lithe form attracted some startled glances, but several ladies, who had previously been anxious to display bosoms like a pouter pigeon and well-rounded shoulders and elbows, had compared themselves with Harriet Stanton and immediately decided themselves to be plump and put themselves on a strict régime.

Harriet had been about to ride out when the lawyer arrived, and her hat, veil and riding-crop lay on a nearby table. The pale winter light falling through the window struck her brown hair, and hinted at red lights in it. "I should like to know how anyone is to be optimistic, when about to be thrown out of one's own home?"

A militant sparkle entered her eyes, and the specu-
lative glance she threw at the riding-crop suggested she
would like physically to set about anyone rash enough
to attempt to carry out this dreadful deed.

"The entail..." the lawyer murmured unhappily.
"There is no way round it, Harriet. Your late father
and I discussed it many times. If there was any way,
any way at all, of preserving Monkscombe in your
possession, believe me, I should have found it. There
isn't," he concluded simply. "It must pass intact,
house, estate and revenue thereof, to the next male
heir. Harr-um... Of course, had your father himself
had the fortune to have a son, this sad state of affairs
would not have arisen. A son would either have inherited, or acted together with his father to cut off the
entail by one of the legal devices... As it was, your
father could hardly..." He cast her an apologetic and
slightly apprehensive look.

If her father had had a son... and not just a pair of
daughters. It had not been for want of trying. Harriet
had been her parents' first-born. They had greeted her
arrival with pleasure, trusting that the next would be
a boy. But it had been another seven years of alter-
nating hope and disappointment before Mrs. Stanton
was once again of a girl. Her confinement had been so
fraught with danger that the doctors had been quite
firm: no more children. Suddenly the Stantons saw
themselves faced with the alarming prospect of the
entail taking Monkscombe and the revenue it represented out of their immediate family altogether,
meaning destitution for Mr. Stanton's widow and his
daughters, should he predecease them all. Neither Mr.
nor Mrs. Stanton had any other private fortune. They

depended entirely upon his estate, to which the entail was so firmly fixed.

As it turned out, Mrs. Stanton died first. Mr. Stanton, though grieving sincerely and no longer a young man, seriously contemplated taking a second wife, with the hope, even at this late stage, of fathering an heir male of his body. Regretfully, he decided it would be too much of a gamble. The sole result might be to leave another widow without support, and, quite possibly, with even more daughters.

In desperation, Mr. Stanton had set himself the goal of living as long as possible, at least long enough to see both his daughters married. But in that, too, he had been frustrated. While carrying out his duties as Justice of the Peace, he had contracted gaol fever from a prisoner, and had died the previous year, leaving both girls unmarried, and unprovided for. Everything had passed immediately into the possession of the son of his younger brother, who had emigrated to what were then the American colonies, but was now the infant United States of America, many years before, as the result of a family quarrel. The brothers had never communicated in any way. Now enquiry revealed that the emigrant, after several adventures, had married and settled in Philadelphia, where he had died some years previously. His son, Benjamin Curtis Stanton, had been born there, and as far as the English Stantons knew, had never set foot in his ancestral homeland. To Benjamin Curtis Stanton, Monkscombe now belonged, lock, stock and barrel.

"Why Curtis?" asked Harriet suddenly now, seemingly at random, but in fact following a pattern of thought in her head.

"I understand," said Mr. Ferrar, clearing his throat and shifting uncomfortably in his chair—confound that jolting chaise—"that Curtis was his mother's family name, and they were anxious to preserve it."

"Hardly tactful, when his entire fortune is to come to him from this side of the family," said Harriet bitterly.

"No one was to know that then, Harriet," he said reprovingly. "Nor, as I understand it, is there any question of Monkscombe being his entire fortune. He has, I believe, a very respectable income of his own, from a successful business founded by his father. And that, dear child, is where we may have some hope. After all, if Mr. Benjamin Stanton does not depend on his English inheritance, he may well see his way to settling some allowance from it upon his cousins. After all, the fellow may be a colonial—I suppose one ought to say American, but even after all this time, a man of my age has great difficulty in thinking of them as anything but the colonies—he may be an American, then, but one can still hope he is a gentleman. Common decency, surely, will urge him to do something for you, and for Caroline."

"It is Caroline who concerns me," Harriet said quietly. "For myself, I can manage somehow. But Caroline..."

Her listener understood her perfectly. Caroline Stanton, at nineteen, was the prettiest girl for miles around, and well aware of it. There was not an eligible male in the county who had not at some time or other fallen in love with her. Caroline was accustomed to receive the adulation of all about her, and accepted it with charming insouciance. In vain had Harriet tried to impress on her younger sister that they had little personal fortune. Living at Monkscombe with a staff of fifteen and every comfort to hand, Caroline had simply discounted Harriet's warnings. Even now, when they were on the verge of losing it all, she still could not be brought to realise that very soon she would no longer be Miss Caroline Stanton of Monkscombe, but just another pretty girl of modest fortune, living in straitened circumstances in rented rooms somewhere. After all, they had been living on here at Monkscombe since their father's death only because it had taken so long to track down Benjamin Stanton.

"Have you found him yet?" Harriet asked wearily. Through the window, she could see the lawn and the bridge over the river, where as a child she had paddled and muddied her gowns. It had been a happy childhood. Now the sight of it all, and the knowledge that it was her home no longer, made the memories too painful to contemplate. Within herself, she felt despair to the point of physical nausea.

"I have hopes," said Mr. Ferrar. "We know he is travelling in Europe. I sent letters to him at Vienna. He should have received them. Unfortunately, the French army is currently in occupation of that city, and it is very difficult to get any reply. One supposes Mr. Stanton is still there, but he could be anywhere. One moment he is at The Hague, the next in Paris, lately in Vienna. The fellow is indefatigable."

"But I don't understand it," Harriet exclaimed. "We are at war with France. The whole of Europe is at war, yet my cousin seems simply to be making the Grand Tour as if nothing were amiss!"

"The United States is not at war with France, Harriet. There is absolutely no reason why he should not pass freely about Europe. He has no doubt armed himself prudently with American papers, and they will give him free passage anywhere. If he wants to make a personal call on Napoleon Bonaparte he may do so, if the fancy takes him.'' This notion appealed to the lawyer's humour, and he gave a short, rasping chuckle, and began to fumble in the pocket of his waistcoat for his snuffbox.

''I see, and if the fancy also takes him, he will include Monkscombe and England on his itinerary, and claim his inheritance!''

''We cannot refuse to let him in,'' said Mr. Ferrar, tapping out a little snuff on the back of his hand. ''In fact, the sooner—'' sniff-sniff ''—he arrives, the better—'' sniff ''—because the sooner we can sort out some practical solution. A-tchoo!''

''By practical solution,'' Harriet said calmly, ''you mean, the sooner Caro and I can throw ourselves on the charity of this, this backwoodsman, and beg to be allowed to live in a couple of unneeded rooms in the least-used wing of what was once our own home! It's unthinkable, Mr. Ferrar! I couldn't face the humiliation—and as for Caro... Yet if I thought that were the answer, I would force myself to do it; to beg Benjamin Curtis Stanton for a home here. But how could Caro be brought to see that she was not still Miss Caroline Stanton of Monkscombe, if still living under this roof? She would carry on as before, behaving as though she owned the place—and I doubt our colonial cousin would put up with that for very long!''

Mr. Ferrar had his own thoughts on the behaviour of Caroline Stanton, but before he could express them, there came a tap on the door and a maid put her head round. ''There's a cap'n of the militia here, Miss

Stanton, and wanting to see you most particular. What shall I do with 'un?''

"Of militia?'' exclaimed the lawyer, showing interest, and thrusting away the large handkerchief in which he had buried his face. "Something amiss?''

"Show him in,'' said Harriet to the maid. "I hope you don't mind, Mr. Ferrar. I don't suppose it will take more than a few minutes. They are always chasing after smugglers, you know, and coming to ask if they may search the grounds.''

A resolute male footstep was heard outside the door, which swung open to admit a stocky young man in a red coat, holding his hat in his hand. His aspect was pleasantly pugnacious, and his youthful features were flushed and showed a curious mixture of anticipation, embarrassment and dogged determination. He glanced quickly about the room, as if he expected—or hoped—to see one person in particular there. That person was obviously missing, because disappointment clearly augmented the other emotions printed on his open countenance. However, he made the best of it, bowed to Harriet, nodded to the lawyer, and made his excuses for having disturbed them.

"It is Captain Murray, is it not?'' said Harriet graciously, holding out her hand. "You have called on us before. Not smugglers again, Captain?''

"Afraid not, ma'am, though smugglers have a hand in it,'' he said, "We're hunting a French spy, Miss Stanton.''

"Good Lord!'' exclaimed the lawyer.

"Yes, sir,'' the young man turned towards him. "We know he was landed along this coast yesterday evening, probably by smugglers. They don't mind whose money they take, and Bonaparte's is as good as any to them. They will have made a rendezvous with a French ship of the line out at sea and taken off their man, landing him under cover of darkness near here.''

"Damn traitors!" exclaimed Mr. Ferrar wrathfully.

"Yes, sir. And I won't be satisfied until every last one of them is hanging on the gallows at Bristol!" said their visitor pugnaciously, thrusting out his chin. "Begging your pardon, Miss Stanton," he added, obviously feeling he had been carried away by zeal for his duty, "but it's catching them red-handed..." Despondency touched his young voice. "Anyway, Miss Stanton, the fellow we're after is known as Lesage, though that might or might not be his right name. We've sealed up the district, tight as a drum, and we don't think he's given us the slip—though he did last night..." Again gloom entered his voice.

Captain Murray had an ambition. It was to capture a notorious felon—a spy would do excellently—and capture him preferably single-handed, thereby would do excellently—and capture him preferably single-handed, thereby becoming a hero, with his name in the gazette, promotion assured and winning *her* heart outright. *She* would be impressed by a hero. She...

"Captain?" enquired Harriet.

Captain Murray started and realised, blushing furiously, that he had drifted off into his favourite daydream. He plunged into renewed speech, to make up for his lapse. "Well, ma'am, he has to be hiding up somewhere, especially during the hours of daylight. The grounds of Monkscombe would be very handy, only a mile from the cove where he landed. My men are on their way here now, ma'am, and I rode on ahead, to give you fair warning and to ask your permission to search."

"Of course," Harriet agreed. "Have you a description of the man?"

"Little enough, but better than nothing," the Captain screwed up his face judiciously. "He's aged about thirty, very tall, six-footer, strong, speaks excellent English, though possibly with a slight accent. He's as clever as a cartload of monkeys, utterly ruthless, and should either you or Miss Caroline encounter him, I beg you, ma'am, to take no risks!"

Real anxiety touched his voice as he mentioned Caroline, and the lawyer looked up quickly and curiously.

"I shall warn the servants," said Harriet. "Thank you, Captain."

This was clearly dismissal, but the young man stood his ground, shuffling his booted feet a little on the parquet. "I feel it my duty, Miss Stanton, to warn Miss Caroline as well."

"I'll tell my sister," Harriet assured him.

He swallowed desperately. "I ought to do it myself, that is..."

Mr. Ferrar took pity on him. "Might it not be a good idea, Harriet, since the Captain is obliged to await his men here, if he went and told Caroline all about it, while you and I finished up our business?"

"I suppose so," said Harriet. "My sister is in the music-room, Captain Murray. One of the servants..."

But Captain Murray was already on his way.

"Pleasant young fellow," Mr. Ferrar remarked.

"Dear Mr. Ferrar," Harriet said drily, "if you imagine I am so blind I don't see that the poor boy is head over heels in love with Caro, you are mistaken! He has called twice to warn us of smugglers. Once to tell us to make sure all our windows were barred because there have been outbreaks of thieving. Once on a most peculiar errand involving stolen horses—which couldn't possibly concern us—and three other times for no reason that I could fathom. It would be extremely unkind of me to encourage him. You know my sister as well as I do. She is the most accomplished flirt. With some young men it doesn't matter, but with that one, it does. He is serious. She is not. If she were to become serious, it would be even worse. I doubt he has more than his soldier's pay, and she, as we both very well know, has no fortune at all other than her looks. He couldn't possibly keep Caro in the manner to which she is accustomed."

"Caroline," said Mr. Ferrar with some asperity, "is going to have to face the fact that her life is about to change. She will have to accustom herself to a retrenched style of living, and that's that."

"She can't," Harriet said. "Her idea of economy is to order two new ball gowns instead of three. She has nobly offered to have them trimmed with Nottingham instead of Flanders lace. Captain Murray may have had a hand in that—I fancy he told her that the Flanders lace was almost certainly smuggled, and the profit from it went into the French war effort."

"Then the young fellow has at least some good influence with her," observed Mr. Ferrar, rising stiffly to his feet. "My dear, you must take this matter of a spy at large seriously. The fellow is on the run, hunted, and it's a hanging matter. He will be dangerous. Watch out. The grounds of Monkscombe—" he gestured towards the window, "are full of thickets of trees and overgrown corners. A wanted man could hide up there very well."

Harriet accompanied him to the chaise, her hat and veil in her hand, and stood in the chill breeze, grateful for the snugly fitting little jacket of the riding-habit. She watched the elderly man climb up awkwardly into his conveyance. She knew how much the journey troubled him, and was grateful for his kindness in coming to see them himself. He could have delegated the whole matter to a younger partner, but he had been her father's friend, and he kept an avuncular eye on them both. He could do nothing about the entail, but he was doing his best for the Stanton girls, all the same. He was a staunch friend, and she had few others to turn to.

Leaning from the chaise, he said unexpectedly, "You're a finer-looking woman than your sister, Harriet. That riding-habit is very fetching, very fetching indeed... I must apologise for arriving as I did, to prevent you from riding out today. You must turn a few heads younger than mine! Oh, Caroline is a pretty girl, I don't deny, but that kind of prettiness won't last for ever. You are handsome, and have the kind of looks that do last. Caroline takes people's eyes; they notice her. But, for my money, you're the best-looking Stanton of them all!" He pressed her hand and raised it gallantly to his lips.

"Bless you, Jonas... You have been a veritable tower of strength to us this past year, since Father died," Harriet told him, with deep and unfeigned gratitude.

He shook his head. He wore an old-fashioned powdered wig. In all her life she had never seen him without one, and often wondered if it was the same one, or

whether it had been renewed exactly identically.
"No," he said, "I'm not the one you need. Too old,
eh! You need a young man to lean on, Harriet."

To himself, he was thinking that it was a great pity
that a fine woman like that had no husband. If he
himself had been forty or even thirty years younger...! A husband would not only have provided her
with comfort and support at this difficult time, but
distracted her from purely practical matters to others
more agreeable. Male companionship, too, would have
softened the directness of her manner, her sometimes
brusque way. She could do worse than to take a leaf
out of little Caroline's book—although Caroline
Stanton was a minx and a flirt with a mind which
darted hither and thither like a firefly, and it was high
time some sensible young fellow took her in hand, like
a highly-bred but skittish filly. It would be a great pity
if Caroline's flirtatious and scatterbrain ways drove
away all sensible admirers, and left none but young
gadabouts as bad as herself. The militia captain, the
young Scotsman, had struck Jonas as a level-headed
young fellow. But Harriet disapproved, and indeed, if
there was no money in either family, it would be a very
bad match. A pity.

Jonas disposed a rug about his knees, lifted his hat
and bowed graciously to Harriet, and called to the
man to drive on.

Harriet watched the chaise clatter away over the
frozen ground. It was a long journey for him back to
Bristol, and an uncomfortable one. She was filled with
misgiving at the thought of it. He must be all of sixty-
five, possibly a little more.

She turned towards the house and glanced up at its
familiar grey exterior. It was called Monkscombe be-

cause there had indeed once been a monastery in the locality. Stantons had lived here ever since the middle ages. They had built and rebuilt the house, so that it represented a curious and not unpleasing jumble of architectural styles. The last rebuilding had taken place in the reign of Queen Anne, and among other features, the house had gained a "Widow's Walk"— the strange external gallery high under the eaves from which the sea, a mile distant, could be seen, and which was so named because traditionally the wives of sea-captains paced it, watching for the return of ships overdue. Monkscombe and the whole Stanton family were an integral part of the countryside, its history, its traditions.

Now a new Stanton was coming: a different sort of Stanton from any who had gone before. An American. A man who had no personal link with the house, who understood nothing of its history or what it meant to the community about it. The traditions of the family, the role they had played in the life of the countryside, all would be foreign to him. The chances were that he would care little for them. Why, there were young men from the district gone with the navy to fight the French—yet Benjamin Curtis Stanton came from a country not even hostile to Bonaparte. He was an outsider, a foreigner, himself. The very thought of him filled Harriet with a dull rage.

"All this," she muttered fiercely, "because Caro and I are women, and the entail demands a male heir! An Englishman's home is said to be his castle! Well, that may be true of Englishmen, but it certainly isn't true of Englishwomen. The law of England has no compunction in making us homeless!"

Feeling as she did, she was unwilling to return at once to the house. She should, of course, make her way directly to the music-room and break up whatever tête-à-tête Captain Murray had succeeded in establishing with her sister. It was not to protect Caro that she should do this, but the unfortunate Captain. The sense of rebellion which had filled her at the thought of the American was extended to include Captain Murray. Good heavens, she was not responsible for that young man! She could not prevent his falling in love any more than she could prevent Caro breaking his heart.

"Ten minutes," she thought. "I'll give them ten minutes more, and if his men haven't arrived by then, I'll go in and sit myself down between them anyway, and put a stop to his lovemaking!"

Harriet jammed the hat on her brown curls, tied the veil under her chin and, blissfully unaware that its jaunty tilt gave her a dashing and slightly rakish air, set off across the lawn, lifting her skirts free of the damp grass. She was not quite sure why she chose this direction, except that she had been gazing at the bridge from the window as she spoke with Jonas and felt herself drawn down there, perhaps because its slightly gloomy air of romantic melancholy blended well with her present mood. As she walked, the memory of the lawyer's parting words came into her head, and although alone, she blushed slightly. She had never been accustomed to think of herself as a beauty, nor did she think of herself now as anything but of reasonable appearance. Caroline had always been the beauty of the family. She supposed Jonas Ferrar was being kind to her, and it would be extremely vain of her to take his words seriously. She felt a little guilty now, dwelling on them.

Harriet sighed. Only a few years ago everything had seemed so simple. Both she and Caroline would marry, everyone assumed it. But now Harriet was twenty-six, and although she had not lacked admirers, none of them had ever remotely attracted her as a possible husband. Caroline, on the other hand, had seemed set to make a brilliant match, despite a lack of personal fortune. She was pretty and vivacious and Monks-combe Park was a respectable background, even entailed. But Caroline was also very young. It had amused her to play ducks and drakes with the hearts of several very eligible young men, and now, suddenly, the tables were turned. Caro did not realise it, but she was no longer in a position to play the flirt.

The bridge was mossy and crumbling and needed repair. There was a great deal about Monkscombe which needed repair, but that was no longer their responsibility. The continued non-appearance of Benjamin Stanton did, however, raise many problems concerning the upkeep of the house and estate. The servants had all been kept on and everything left as it had been at her father's death, but could not be kept so indefinitely. Sooner or later Benjamin Stanton had to be contacted and persuaded to give some orders. As things stood, no one, at the moment, had any authority to do anything.

"Wretched man!" exclaimed Harriet aloud. "He is a complete nuisance in every way. Now, I suppose, he is bottled up in Vienna, hob-nobbing with the French, and quite prepared to let Monkscombe fall down before he deigns to come and inspect it! He will put in an appearance when he sees fit, probably wearing buck-skin and 'chawing 'baccy'!''

This mental image gave her a certain grim satisfaction. She crossed over the bridge and entered the coppice beyond. Beneath a large old yew-tree, she stopped and fell to ruminating, thinking how calm it was and how it almost made her unquiet mind more peaceful.

A sudden sound, like a rifle shot, echoed on the crisp air. For a split second Harriet even took it for a gun, discharged carelessly close at hand. Instinct made her leap backwards, almost losing her balance as, with a rending of branches, a heavy body crashed through the yew above her and plummeted to her feet. Harriet gave a shriek, then clasped her hand to her mouth cutting off the cry in the middle.

Silence followed her exclamation, a strange, suspended and artificial silence. The birds had fled, and Harriet, her heart pounding painfully in her chest almost as if it would leap out, saw, lying before her, spread-eagled on his back, a strange man.

The fall appeared to have knocked him unconscious. For a dreadful moment she even thought he might be dead. She crept forward hesitantly and stooped over him. He was a complete stranger, a big, strong fellow, his long arms and legs flung out awkwardly, covering the ground between the trees. She had no idea who he could be, but for the moment this seemed less important than the possibility that he might be seriously injured. Harriet dropped to her knees on the damp ground, heedless of the damage to her habit, and hesitantly put out a hand to touch his brow. To her immense relief, and some alarm, he stirred and groaned.

She took her hand away quickly. At least he was not dead, and he was coming round. His light brown hair, worn a little long, had fallen back from his face, revealing a high forehead and lean features, all tanned to an unseasonable walnut hue, surely from buffeting by wind and weather, rather than from the sun, in this November month of 1805. He had travelled here, most likely by horseback, unshielded from the elements. As she studied him, his eyes opened unexpectedly and were revealed to be a blue-grey. Their gaze, as he fought to focus on her face, was at first a little hazy, but slowly cleared. He puckered his eyebrows and scowled.

Harriet had regained her presence of mind. She scrambled to her feet and stood back, as clear of him as was possible among the dark treetrunks. He struggled into an upright sitting position and put one hand gingerly to the crown of his head.

"Are you all right?" she whispered. It seemed the obvious question.

The stranger gave a non-committal grunt, which might have meant either yes or no, and squinted up at her in the shaft of pale winter sunlight that now fell across his face. The grey eyes were suddenly shrewd. He lurched forward and got to his feet. He was extraordinarily tall. She had not fully realised it when he had been lying flat on the ground. Now he seemed enormous. Harriet herself was of no more than middle height for a woman of her time, which was far from tall, and now felt rather like one of those hapless humans in a fairy-tale who finds she has wandered into a land of giants.

She stepped back prudently, and with an outward composure she was very far from feeling inside, demanded sternly, "Who are you? You're trespassing."

"On whose land?" he challenged, peering down at her. His voice had a curious inflection to it, which she could not quite place.

She was about to reply "On ours!", when she recalled that it was not theirs, not any more. "On the Monkscombe estate!" she said angrily.

He did not look impressed. "What are you?" he asked, rather rudely.

"I am Harriet Stanton!" she almost shouted, growing even angrier. "Will you explain what you are doing here—and up a tree?" The ridiculous aspect of it struck her and added embarrassment to her anger.

He rubbed his chin and surveyed her thoughtfully, without replying, as if he debated what he should say. At that moment an idea struck Harriet, so horrific that it almost paralysed her. He was the French spy! Lesage, or whatever he was called. What had Murray said? Six-footer—yes, all of that. Strongly built—yes. Slight accent—yes, he did have some sort of accent.

Carefully she said, "You really have no business here, but you have taken a very bad fall. If you come up to the house, you may have a glass of wine to restore you."

He seemed relieved that she had not pressed him for his identity. "Why, that's a very fine notion," he said appreciatively. "Thank'ee, ma'am."

She had thought he might be more difficult to persuade than this, and was rather taken aback by the way in which he simply turned and set off towards the bridge over the river, and the direction of the house. He walked with a long, loping stride, and she was forced almost to trot alongside him in an effort to keep up. "Why," she asked, curiosity overcoming prudence, "were you in a tree?"

"Because, like Zacchaeus, I wanted to observe and not be seen."

But Miss Stanton had also been to Bible class. "Zacchaeus was very small. That's why he did it. I suppose he didn't weigh very much. You weigh much too much—and are far too big, and too old, to go climbing trees. It's a most dangerous and silly thing to do," she finished severely.

"I have done many dangerous things in my time, Miss Harriet. That was the least of them." He paused. They were near to the house now. "The chaise is gone," he said. "But you have another visitor." He pointed to the riding-horse which a groom held before the front door.

"Oh, you need pay no attention to that," she replied hastily, hoping he was not close enough to notice the militia saddlecloth. "It is a young man who has called on my sister."

So he had indeed been watching the house! It made her feel distinctly uncomfortable, and even a little frightened. With what purpose had he waited so patiently in the coppice?

"Anyone else at home?" he enquired. For all his easy tone, there was an edge to his voice. The question was serious.

"Only the servants." Harriet ushered him through a side door and into the hall. "Of course, if you are hurt, I could send for the surgeon."

"No!" he said sharply.

"Just as you wish," she soothed him. She opened the music-room door.

Captain Murray was actually on his knees. He looked, poor fellow, as though he were in the middle of proposing. Caroline, seated on a stool and clasping a sheet of music, was watching him with mild interest. Both looked up as Harriet appeared.

"Captain Murray!" cried Harriet urgently. The Captain began to scramble guiltily to his feet, obviously casting about for some excuse for his posture. Before he could speak, Harriet flung out a hand and, seizing her companion by the sleeve to stop his escaping, gasped, "I found this man in the coppice. He fell out of a tree. I'm sure he is your spy, Lesage!"

For a moment the unfortunate Captain seemed thunderstruck. In all his many daydreams of heroic action he had never been discovered at the vital moment, on his knees before his beloved, with his sword-belt unbuckled and hanging on the edge of a nearby chair. But he was an enterprising young man, and quick witted. He made a dive for his sword-belt, dragged out the weapon and brandishing it in a warlike manner, declared breathlessly, "Explain yourself, sir—or I shall arrest you!"

"Goodness, James," murmured Caroline with some awe.

Captain Murray grew in stature. Now things were turning out as he had planned. "Don't move!" he ordered threateningly, approaching the stranger with caution.

Caroline Stanton turned her wide blue eyes on the newcomer. Her gaze was slightly myopic, but not so that anyone noticed. Her full lips were partly open as if she had been waiting to be kissed, and her puzzled face was framed in a cloud of coppery coloured curls. She had already abandoned mourning grey for mauve, because she looked better in mauve. At this precise moment, she was rather pleased to think she looked well. They seldom received visits from interesting strangers. She smiled charmingly upon this one, and asked, "Who are you?"

"Wait a bit, Caroline!" ordered Captain Murray crossly. "Let me handle this. I'll ask him! Sir, have you means of identification?"

"In my pocket," said Harriet's prisoner amiably. He put a hand towards his coat, and paused. "Ah—you will be afraid I might produce a loaded pistol."

Captain Murray, trying to look as if he had thought of this, ordered, "Keep your hands where I can see them! Miss Stanton, perhaps you would oblige?"

"In my inside pocket, Miss Harriet," said their prisoner with the familiarity he had shown before, "you will find some papers—if you would be so kind."

Harriet gingerly stretched out her hand and removed a folded wad of papers from the pocket he indicated. She held them out towards Captain Murray.

The Captain found himself in something of a dilemma. He could not take the papers and peruse them without lowering his sword. "You read them, Miss Stanton!" he requested.

Harriet opened them out, read a few lines, and uttered a strangled gasp, followed by a low moan.

"Oh, Harriet, whatever is wrong?" cried Caroline, seeing that her sister had turned deathly pale.

"No," Harriet said in a dull, obstinate voice. "No, it is quite impossible!" Suddenly she turned on the man beside her and burst out, "You wretch, you have stolen these papers!"

"My signature is on them," he said. "I'll sign again, and you can compare the two, if you like. No, I'm afraid I haven't stolen them. Nor am I the French spy you seem to think you have caught. Please put up that weapon, Captain. Miss Harriet—pass the Captain my papers."

Dumbly, Harriet obeyed his orders. Captain Murray snatched them from her and cast an eye over them hurriedly. Then he looked up, his honest face flushed and embarrassed. "Why," he said angrily, "these say your name is Stanton!"

"So it is," said the newcomer, unperturbed. "Ben Stanton—and this I know is cousin Harriet—so you," he smiled at Caroline, who dimpled attractively, to Captain Murray's increased fury, "so you are my cousin Caroline." He walked into the middle of the music-room, watched in silence by the three of them. "And this," he said, gesturing widely at the room and its contents, "is my house." The grey eyes surveyed them, their expression challenging a denial. "Well, is no one going to welcome me home?"

CHAPTER TWO

COMPLETE SILENCE followed Ben Stanton's last words. Eventually Harriet, still unable to accept the evidence of the papers, stammered, "But you cannot... You, that is, he, is in Vienna!"

"Was in Vienna," he corrected her. "And a very fine city it is. Unfortunately at the moment it is under occupation, and crowded out with the soldiers of the Grand Army. They are billeted on virtually every citizen and occupy every café, theatre seat and place of entertainment to be found. I don't say that some of their officers aren't excellent company, but there were just too many people around for my liking. The lawyer—Ferrar, isn't it?—has been pursuing me across Europe with letters, so I thought now is the time to go to England and spend a little time in the countryside, enjoying some peace and quiet. Of course, I hadn't anticipated being arrested."

"Sir," said Captain Murray hoarsely. "You have been fraternising with the enemy!"

"Not my enemy, Captain. The United States is not at war with France. In fact, we think very kindly of the French. Lafayette, you recall."

Typically, it was Caroline who broke the frozen tableau they had formed until then. She jumped up enthusiastically from her music-stool and ran towards Stanton, seizing his hands. "But it's such an

adventure! You have seen the French army—and did
you see Bonaparte? Only think, you've come at last,
and we've been waiting and waiting for you! We had
no idea what you would be like, or how you looked,
and Harriet was so convinced you would be quite
primitive, a sort of backwoodsman, and wear leather
clothes, and . . ." At this point, even Caroline seemed
to realise these indiscretions were potentially disas-
trous, and left unspoken the further revelations on her
lips. She turned towards the other two and, beaming
and still clasping Stanton's hand, exclaimed, "There,
and we were all so worried—and he's very nice, after
all, and perfectly civilised."

"I've no wish," said Captain Murray in a strangled
voice, "to interfere in a family matter. But it occurs to
me, Miss Stanton, that Mr. Ferrar can't be very far on
the road, not in that hired chaise. It seems to me, if
you'll forgive me, that he ought to be here. Perhaps I
should ride after him, and bring him back?"

Harriet managed to pull herself together. "Yes,
Captain, that's an excellent idea, and thank you so
much. Caro, let go of—of Mr. Benjamin Stanton's
hand at once!"

The Captain took himself off with a clatter of boots,
and Caroline released Ben Stanton rather reluctantly.
Harriet had no intention of letting the situation slip
out of her control entirely, so she caught her sister by
the arm and hustled her out of the room with the in-
structions to tell the housekeeper to make up a room
for the new arrival, and then turned back to Stanton.

He had walked over to the window and was gazing
out at the grounds. She stared hard at his averted form
and wondered whether it would be best to tackle him
here and now, or to wait for Jonas Ferrar to return.

Before she could speak, however, her cousin began to talk. He seemed to be talking as much to himself as to her, in a low voice, which she had to strain her ears to catch, since he kept his back turned to her.

"It's a curious thing to be here. My father used to talk about this house. He described it to me so often, and so well, that I always felt I knew it. I dare say you find this very odd, but I don't feel I come here as a stranger."

"Then I really fail to understand," Harriet said, "why you couldn't arrive at the front door like any normal person."

He hesitated, then turned towards her at last. "I couldn't be sure of my reception." He sounded a little hesitant, and, for the first time, awkward. "I thought it best to spy out the land first. The fact of the matter is, I always intended to include a visit to Monkscombe on my trip to Europe. I vaguely thought I might come incognito—in case I wasn't welcome. I knew my father had quarrelled with his family, and I wasn't quite sure whether that quarrel had been forgotten with the passage of time—or if it was remembered and still alive. Then, when I reached The Hague, I received the first of Ferrar's letters, and learned, to my complete surprise—and I can tell you, to some consternation—that I had inherited the place."

Harriet sat down on the stool vacated by Caroline and surveyed him suspiciously. "You didn't acknowledge that letter. Mr. Ferrar has been writing to addresses all over Europe."

He moved away from the window, and stood looking down at her with his hands behind his back. "I didn't acknowledge it, cousin, because if I had done so, Ferrar would have expected me to arrive in En-

gland by the first available packet. That wasn't—
practicable—at the time. Anyway, I needed time to
think about the changed situation.''

"Time?'' Harriet exclaimed, unable to control her
resentment. ''It has been over a year since Father died,
and more than six months since we discovered that you
were in Europe! Have you any idea what is involved in
running an estate the size of Monkscombe? Can you
imagine what it has been like, with no one able to take
a single decision, because the owner was gallivanting
about Europe and didn't care whether the house fell
down? Do you realise the responsibilities that owner-
ship of this house carries? Have you thought about the
tenants. Have you thought about the servants? They
have all been living for the past year on tenterhooks.''

An obstinate expression had crossed his face as she
spoke. He said defiantly, ''The house looks solid
enough to me, and the servants all seem to be in em-
ployment.''

"Mr. Stanton,'' Harriet exploded, beside herself,
"As far as I am concerned, you have behaved extremely badly. The very least you could have done
would have been to let us know your intentions. I
don't believe you have the slightest notion of what in-
heriting Monkscombe means. Nor do I believe the
sentimental story you spun me just now, about your
father and your wish to visit us. I don't know why you
were hiding in the coppice, but your explanation of
that is equally unlikely. I am assuming for the moment that you are indeed Benjamin Stanton, as you
claim, but apart from that, whatever you are, you are
certainly not a gentleman, neither do you have the re-
motest idea of how a gentleman behaves! You appear
to me a most ill-bred and vulgar fellow!''

She knew, as she spoke, that her words were likely to make him angry, but even so, she was unprepared for what followed.

"That's enough!" he ordered loudly and so sharply that her voice died in her throat. The grey eyes glittered at her and the lean features set into rigid lines. Beneath the bronze, his face was drained of all colour and his whole face seemed a mask of anger. He pointed a finger at her and added, "I mean it, Harriet! Now, I'm an easy-going fellow when folk play fair by me—but a bad one to cross, as they very quickly find if they don't! What's more, I'm not a fool. I know you don't want me here. I know you don't want me to have Monkscombe, and I'm well aware that I should not be its owner had your parents not had the bad luck to produce only daughters." He saw colour flood her face and heard her gasp. "Oh yes, Miss Harriet. You may have been totally ignorant of my existence, but I have not been quite so ignorant of yours! Over the years, friends and correspondents in England kept first my father, and then me, well informed as to developments in our family here. Now, I understand how you feel. You're accustomed to look on this house as your home. I'm prepared to make allowances for your being upset. I'm even prepared to apologise for alarming you by falling out of a tree and for arriving generally in an unorthodox manner. But the fact is that I enter this house as of right. This is my house. I am its master, and I am the head of this family. I shall be making all future decisions as to what is done here. Why, if I decide to empty the place and close it up, I shall do so!"

Harriet paled. "You are obliged to administer it to the best advantage possible. That responsibility is laid upon you."

"I shall do so. I fancy I know a great deal more than my English relatives about running businesses profitably. I, you see, never depended on inherited wealth. We American Stantons made all our money ourselves, by soiling our hands with trade."

"Profit!" She looked as though Stanton had uttered an indecency.

"That shocks you, does it? Well, you will have to get used to the unpleasant idea. You will have to get used to a great many things. In short, Miss Harriet, I shall do whatever I like here, and neither you nor Caroline has any say in the matter. Is that understood?"

She rose to her feet, shaking in every limb and yet so obviously determined to maintain her dignity that he had to admire her, for all he was so angry. Most women would have burst into tears and run out of the room by now. He felt a spasm of compunction at having been so outspoken, but he need not have worried.

"I see," Harriet managed to say in a tolerably even voice. "I shall make arrangements to remove both my sister and myself at the earliest possible opportunity. Until then, we shall do our best not to get in your way. You can give your orders directly to the housekeeper. Her name is Woods, and she is a very competent woman. Mr. Ferrar—who should be on his way back here now, if Captain Murray has been able to catch him—is not only our lawyer, but the land agent for the estate. He can tell you all the details."

He sighed, and raised a placating hand. "See here, Miss Harriet, I lost my temper. Of course, you and Caroline will stay here, for as long as you like. Where would you go?"

"That is not your concern, Mr. Stanton."

"At least," he burst out irritably, his anger welling up again, "stop calling me 'Mr. Stanton'! We're cousins, for pity's sake!"

"So *you* say," Harriet told him.

"Don't start that again. Wait till the lawyer gets here and let him be the judge." For a moment he seemed to struggle with some obstacle in his own mind, and eventually added a little gruffly, "Harriet, you must know perfectly well that I can't just walk in here and run this house, with or without the excellent Mrs. Woods." He drew a deep breath. "Now, you would oblige me very much if you would remain and—and do whatever you have been doing up till now by way of running the place."

In the circumstances, it was a handsome admission on his part, and it cost him a great deal to make it. They stared at each other. It was an impasse, and both knew it. If she walked out now, he would be left with a first-rate muddle on his hands. On the other hand, she had nowhere to go, and he knew it.

Harriet sat down again and folded her hands in her lap. "Then we shall wait for Jonas, for Mr. Ferrar. If I might be permitted to make a suggestion, with regard to him?"

"Please do," Stanton said with icy politeness.

"He is an elderly man, and rather rheumaticky. The journey here shook him up most dreadfully. Now he's had to turn back and make half of it again. I really don't think we... That is, I feel that *you* should not send him all the way to Bristol tonight. We, that is, you, can easily put him up here at Monkscombe overnight."

"Thank you," Stanton said. "I'll suggest it to Ferrar."

WHEN DAWN BROKE GREYLY over Monkscombe the following morning, it did so over a household in which it was doubtful that anyone had slept very well. The servants were all agog with the arrival of the new master. Gossip in the servants' hall was rife as to what he meant to do. Mr. Ferrar, the lawyer, they told one another, had stayed overnight, and that, surely, meant something.

Mr. Ferrar himself was making his way down to the music-room, a full hour before breakfast, in response to an urgent note that had been delivered to him with the hot water. He straightened his wig before he went in, and wondered if it would not have been better to have handed over this whole business to a younger man, after all. Not that he wished to abandon Harriet Stanton, but Harriet's devotion to Monkscombe and its future, far from being shaken by the arrival of the heir, seemed to have been redoubled. She was in the music-room ahead of him, pacing up and down. She had, he noticed, laid aside her half-mourning in favour of a dark blue gown. A new era had dawned at Monkscombe.

"Well, my dear?" he asked wheezily. The early morning air always settled on his chest. He seated himself and patted his waistcoat absently for his snuffbox, before remembering that he had left it on the wash-stand. Tiresome, he thought.

"I'm sorry to have brought you down so early," Harriet apologised. She noticed the searching movement of his hands, and asked, "Have you lost something?"

"Nothing. Nothing of importance," he said regretfully. "Left upstairs... It can wait. Out with it, Harriet, what's on your mind? Ben Stanton, I suppose."

"He is Ben Stanton, then?" she asked doubtfully. "You're quite sure of it?"

"Quite sure, my dear. Quite apart from his papers, which are all in order, he bears a striking resemblance to his late father. You, of course, never knew your uncle, but I did. Remember him well. As a matter of fact, there is still a likeness of him hanging on that wall, just over there." He pointed.

Startled, Harriet went to inspect the miniature in its oval frame. "Is that my uncle? I never knew. No one ever said."

"Family quarrels," Mr. Ferrar said. "There's a resemblance, don't you think?"

"Y-es..." she agreed reluctantly. "Only I couldn't sleep a wink last night, and I began to wonder if, you know, he had stolen the papers." She began to hurry on, seeing protest on his florid face. "After all, Ben Stanton was in Vienna, which is occupied by the French. The papers could have been confiscated from him there, and used by the French to send one of their spies here."

"Believe me, Harriet," Mr. Ferrar said heavily, "that is Ben Stanton."

"Even so..." An obstinate expression crossed her face. "He is very well disposed towards the French. The description Captain Murray gave us of Lesage tallies very well with Ben Stanton's, and it could still be, you know, that he and Lesage are one and the same man. Lesage has not yet been found, and Captain Murray says he's certainly hiding up somewhere under our noses."

"Now look, Harriet!" Mr. Ferrar said sharply, "this has got to stop. I know how you feel about this house. I realise the shock at seeing your cousin, and so unexpectedly. But fancies, which belong better in one of those extraordinary novels that literary ladies seem to pen these days, are best put right out of your head at this minute. Ben Stanton is here, and you have to come to terms with him. Antagonising him by making wild accusations will do no good. Now then, have you had any opportunity to discuss your future, and Caroline's, with him?"

"Hardly any. He says we may stay for as long as we wish—but I don't know that I wish to stay here, if *he* is going to be here. He hasn't the slightest idea, you know, what running this estate means. He seems to think being a country gentleman no different from running a business. No Stanton has ever been in trade, yet he seems to be quite proud of it. He talks about making Monkscombe profitable, and I don't think I could bear to stay here and watch him. I certainly couldn't do it and stay silent! He will cut down all the woodland and put up all the rents. He has the most dreadful temper," she added, slightly at a tangent to her main argument.

"I thought him a very amiable fellow," the lawyer remarked.

"Only when things are going his way. He dislikes to be crossed."

Mr. Ferrar eyed her in silence. The trouble with the girl is, he thought, that she has no idea of how to manage a man. It don't come natural to her. Caroline, I don't doubt, will have Ben Stanton twisted round her little finger in no time. Poor Harriet, I fear, is far too straightforward, and hurtles on to meet obstacles.

"I am to have a discussion with him after breakfast," he said, rising wheezily to his feet. "My advice to you, Harriet, is to leave matters to me."

"You needn't worry that I shall be interrupting," Harriet said rather resentfully. "I shall be taking the gig and driving round after breakfast, making as many calls as I can."

"A little early for making calls, ain't it?" he asked, surprised.

"They are unusual calls. I have to tell everyone that the heir to Monkscombe has arrived. I shall start, I dare say, with the rector, and old Sir Mortimer Fish, and work my way down to the Misses Drew, who will probably fall all a-twitter and offer to send him jars of potted meat by way of a welcome present. It will take me the best part of the day."

"I see. Will Henderson drive you?"

"I am perfectly capable of taking the ribbons myself!" she told him with some asperity.

WELL WRAPPED UP against the chill wind in a fur pelisse, Harriet bowled along in the gig. She handled the horse very capably, as she had told the lawyer. The gig was rather a more dashing vehicle than ladies usually drove. Driving was rather a man's accomplishment, and most young ladies were content to be driven out in a pony-drawn phaeton. The horse was a showy animal too, a bright chestnut with four snowy white socks. Little wonder that Harriet Stanton out driving turned quite a few heads!

She felt much better now that she was in the fresh air. Being in charge of the gig helped, too. It made her feel that at least she controlled something. Events at Monkscombe were rapidly passing right out of her province. She and Caroline could not stay there indefinitely, of that she was gloomily certain. Not if Ben Stanton stayed, at any rate, and he seemed disposed to stay at the moment. Probably eventually he would become bored with being an English squire and move on, or go back to America. Monkscombe and its estate would be left in the hands of an agent, and, when that happened, everything and everyone would suffer. An absentee landlord was the very worst kind.

Her cousin was certainly not altogether what she had expected. She was not quite sure just what she had expected. Caro, of course, had told him they expected a frontiersman with a racoon cap and a musket. He wasn't that. When he had appeared at breakfast, bathed and shaved and in clean linen, he had looked eminently respectable, not to say quite distinguished. At least they could be grateful that he did not reveal obviously that he was in trade. He seemed to have received an excellent education, was extensively travelled, had a clear grasp of his legal rights, and had not the slightest hesitation in making decisions. All in all, he presented a formidable opponent. Harriet was not sure she would not have preferred a simple backwoodsman, after all.

"And I still don't know why he was skulking in the coppice and hiding in a tree!" she said aloud.

The breeze carried her words away. It stung her cheeks and turned them rosy-red. Her brown curls tumbled out from beneath her hat, which was securely tied on with a veil, and anyone seeing her would certainly have agreed with Jonas Ferrar that this was the best-looking Stanton of them all. But Harriet herself was blissfully unaware of it. She turned in at the rectory at a spanking pace.

The rector had just retired to his study to start his next Sunday's sermon. He was startled to see Miss Stanton so early, and even more startled to hear her news. He would call, he promised, upon Mr. Stanton at the earliest opportunity. Would Mr. Stanton feel it injudicious on the rector's part to preach next Sunday on the Return of the Prodigal, as he had intended?

Harriet scrambled back into the gig and bowled along to see Sir Mortimer Fish. He was ancient, deaf and vague, and had to be told three times over. Even then he seemed to confuse Ben Stanton with his father, and saw her away with the words, "I told the boy he wouldn't last out in Pennsylvania. Lot of Quakers. Wouldn't appreciate a bottle of decent port if they saw one, and fit for nothing but singing psalms and making money. I told him he'd be back!"

It was already nearing mid-day, and she wondered if the Misses Drew would be ready to receive visits. They lived in genteel poverty, in a house which belonged to the Monkscombe estate, and for which they paid an extremely low rent. Their father had once been rector there, and although dead over thirty years, his daughters were still guided by what dear papa would have wished.

"Dear Harriet!" cried Miss Drew, waving at her frantically from the garden gate. "Why are you out so early? Is something wrong?"

When Harriet told them, they both became highly excitable and talked across one another.

"We shall leave a card!" said Miss Drew, after some thought. "I think that would be correct, would it not, Mary?"

"Papa would have wished us to do so," said her sister firmly.

"We shall send him a little gift of jam," declared Miss Drew.

"Do gentlemen care much for jam?" asked Miss Mary doubtfully.

"Then potted meat. What do you think, Harriet, would he prefer potted meat? Papa was very partial to potted meat."

"I'm sure he would be very touched, Miss Drew."

"There, then potted meat it shall be. Perhaps jam as well, although that might seem . . ." She cast a doubtful eye at her sister.

"Papa would have wished, Eleanor."

"Then just wait a minute there, Harriet, and I'll have Daisy look out a jar of each, so that you can take them with you."

It's all very well to laugh at the Misses Drew, thought Harriet sadly as she drove away, the jars of jam and potted meat rattling in the bottom of the gig. But there go Caro and myself. If neither of us marries, well, I shan't and it's possible, now, that Caroline might not either . . . We shall end up living in some grace-and-favour house on the estate, making jam and doing good works, just like that.

Preoccupied with these thoughts, she failed to notice that a man was walking along the roadside ahead of her. It was not until she was almost level with him that she became aware of his presence and recognised, with a sinking heart, Aaron Pardy.

Almost every village in England had its family reckoned by all to be "a bad lot", and treated very much as pariahs in the community. In their locality, that position belonged to the Pardys. Pardy was not an uncommon name thereabouts, but respectable Pardys always repudiated any connection with this family. The Pardy family lived in appalling squalor in a pair of tumbledown cottages away from the village and near to the sea. Officially they were fishermen. Unofficially, and everyone knew it, they were smugglers. In the past, one or two had even been wreckers, that worst of crimes, luring ships on to the rocks with false lights, and murdering the few survivors who managed to swim exhausted to shore. Those Pardys had eventually been hanged for their crimes, and nowadays the family stuck to smuggling, counting the risks fewer. No one condoned wrecking, but quite a few people who should have known better condoned smuggling. Many a gentleman paid for French brandy by night at his back door and did not ask whence it came. Many a lady wore French lace and perfumes, acquired in the same way.

The Pardys were a numerous family. The only time they neared a church was when they died and had to be buried somewhere. The babies were seldom baptized, and no one could remember a Pardy getting legally married. They all lived together in a jumble of relationships which were hopelessly confused. The babies, and there were always babies, seemed to belong to everyone, and their exact parentage was almost impossible to disentangle. The men alike were handsome in a coarse way, great drinkers, brawlers and womanisers. The Pardy women were almost all sullen, sluttish, cowed and pregnant.

Of Aaron, Harriet had always been secretly afraid. He was a good-looking, strapping fellow of perhaps five and twenty. He was not, as far as anyone knew, married, even after the common law, which was not to say that one or more of the unwashed children playing in the filth about the Pardy dwellings did not belong to him. He was, in his own manner, a dandy, and it always seemed to Harriet that he looked at her in a way he did not look at anyone else. He was freely spoken, too, and sometimes, if she happened to catch his eye, would wink at her as if they shared some secret. That she was Miss Stanton of Monkscombe did not impress him. Like the celebrated miller of Dee, Aaron Pardy cared for no man, and very few cared for him.

As bad luck would have it, the lane here was narrow and deeply rutted. Harriet was obliged to slow the gig to a walk. At first she hoped Aaron might let her by with no more than an insolent greeting. But as the horse drew level with his shoulder, he raised one arm and grasped the bridle, bringing the gig to a rocking halt.

"Release my horse at once, Aaron!" she ordered furiously.

He grinned at her. "Well, Miss Stanton, as I live and breathe! And pretty as a picture. Driving around to tell them all the news, are you?"

Harriet flushed and jerked unavailingly on the reins. "I've no idea what you're talking about. I said, let go!"

He clicked his tongue in mock reproach. "No idea? Got a new master up at the house, I hear. You'll be going round and telling folks as Mr. Stanton has come over from Ameriky and wants what's his.''

"My cousin, Mr. Benjamin Curtis Stanton, has arrived," she said tersely. "If confirmation of that was all you wanted, you have it, and now you may let me go by."

Aaron stood, still grasping the bridle in one hand and stroking the horse's nose with the other. "You won't be too pleased to see him, I reckon."

"It's no business of yours!" she cried out furiously. "Nor is that true. Of course we were pleased to see him arrive safely."

He chuckled. "That's not what I heard. I heard you tried to turn him over to the soldiers."

"How on earth did you know that?" she gasped. "Who told you?"

Aaron grinned up at her slyly. "Oh, I hears all sorts. I like to keep a eye on you, Miss Stanton, and know what you're doing-of. Might be you'll have need of me, one day."

"I think it extremely unlikely!" she snapped. She pulled on the reins again, and the chestnut flung up its head and backed a few steps. The gig rocked dangerously.

"A bolting horse is a powerful strong beast," Aaron said slowy, his deepset, dark eyes watching her face. "A young lady like yourself couldn't control 'un."

She was truly afraid then, not sure what he meant to do, but believing him capable of anything. Harriet grasped the whip from its socket and struck out at him. She meant only to force him to release the horse, but her aim was truer than she intended and the lash caught him across one unshaven cheek. She saw the red weal appear and heard him swear viciously. He threw up his hand to ward off any further attack, and the chestnut, already nervous and further alarmed by the crack of the whip, leapt forward.

For the next few minutes, Harriet was more frightened than she had been at any time in her life. The chestnut had taken the bit between his teeth. Good driver that she was, Aaron had been right, and she had not the strength to control a bolting horse. The wheels of the gig struck the ruts in the lane and the vehicle bounced high into the air. Harriet grasped at the bodywork to prevent being flung out and waited for them to overturn, as it seemed inevitable that they must.

Somehow, the gig remained upright. The chestnut galloped headlong down the lane, heading for an intersection of roads, and Harriet hauled on the reins helplessly. Amid the noise, confusion and panic, she became aware that a horse and rider had appeared ahead of her and blocked the path. The chestnut reared up, mud and grit flew everywhere, the horseman flung out a hand and grasped the chestnut's bridle and the gig came at last to a lurching halt. To her complete dismay, she recognised Ben Stanton.

"Are you hurt?" he asked her sharply.

Dumbly, she shook her head. She was struggling for breath, and her lungs ached. He dismounted and led his horse to the rear of the gig, where he attached it. Then he returned and pulled himself up on the driving-seat beside her, and took the reins from her hands. He flicked them, and the lathered chestnut obediently walked on, too exhausted to play up any more.

"Would you care to explain to me," he said coldly, "why you are driving alone about the countryside in an extremely unsuitable vehicle?"

Harriet had regained sufficient breath. "I always drive myself—the gig is mine. It's not unsuitable."

"You were fortunate not to break your neck."

"It's the first time any such thing has happened!" she cried out angrily. "It wouldn't have done so, if..." She broke off, obscurely ashamed of mentioning Aaron.

"Oh, I saw what happened," he said brusquely. "Who was that fellow?"

"Aaron Pardy," she told him unwillingly. "He's nobody, a local ne'er-do-well."

"For a nobody, he seemed to be a mite familiar!" Harriet flushed. "Pardy," he went on. "Does that make him a member of that family of hillbillies living down by the shore?"

"I don't know what a hillbilly is," she told him, "but they live by the shore in a couple of half-ruined cottages. It's no part of the Monkscombe estate. We can't do anything about them."

"Ferrar was telling me. He's on his way back to Bristol, by the by."

Harriet's heart sank at the thought of Jonas no longer being there to support her. She became aware that something was rolling about in the bottom of the gig and striking her foot. She stooped and gathered up a pot of jam. The potted meat was missing.

"The Misses Drew sent you this," she said, seeing Stanton glance at it. "There was another, potted meat, but it seems to have fallen out. They meant it very kindly!" she added defiantly.

He nodded. "Aren't they tenants of the estate? I was looking over the books with Ferrar. Those two ladies seem to pay very little rent for the property."

"They can't afford any more!" Harriet cried indignantly.

"That's not my concern. As you said yourself, I am obliged to run the estate profitably. I shall look into the matter of the Misses Drew's rent."

"Profitably, not heartlessly!" Harriet almost shouted at him. "The Misses Drew are ladies, their father was rector here, and they are both quite elderly. You cannot propose to turn them out! Where should they go? They have no relations, no one!"

"I can't supply their want of family, Harriet. That seems to be quite a nice little house they have there, and it could fetch a much higher rent."

"If you were a gentleman, you would know that there are other obligations than that of making money!" she told him furiously.

"I am not a gentleman, Miss Harriet. I make no claim to the title. I'm a businessman."

They were within sight of Monkscombe by now. Harriet fell silent, her lips pressed tightly together, not trusting herself to speak. When they had clattered sedately into the stableyard, Stanton jumped down first and politely reached up his hand to help her.

"Now then, Miss Harriet, if you want to drive out again, you'll have one of the hired hands drive you. Is that clear?"

"There—is—no—need," said Harriet tightly, emphasising each word.

"Seems to me, there is. French spies on the loose, militia all over the place, village roughnecks wandering the lanes. Those are my orders, Harriet."

"I do not take your orders!" she snapped furiously.

"If it concerns outside the walls of the house, you most certainly do. I'll leave you to make up menus and so forth with Mrs. Woods, and worry about the laundry. That's women's business, anyway. You just mind what goes on in the kitchen and suchlike, Harriet. Act respectable."

"Respectable!" Harriet shrieked, but he had walked on ahead of her, and her voice echoed back mockingly in the empty hall.

CHAPTER THREE

HARRIET HAD NO WISH to continue their quarrel in front of Caroline, so dinner that evening passed in icy politeness, at least as far as she and Ben Stanton were concerned. Caroline chattered on unconcernedly, asking him endless questions about his travels, to which he replied patiently and good-naturedly enough. He even apologised that he was no expert on ladies' fashions and could tell Caroline little on that score, although it seemed to him that white was very much à la mode among the French ladies and, indeed, in Vienna, too. Though he himself, he added, thought it an insipid colour for a ballgown. "Makes them all look as though they've come down to dance in their nightgowns," he said.

Caroline giggled; Harriet stared stonily at her plate. Once or twice he glanced at her surreptitiously, but each time her gaze was firmly averted.

But now Caroline was taken with the notion of dancing, and began to wheedle him into saying that they might have a musical evening at Monkscombe, "Since we have had no company to speak of since Papa died. Of course, it wasn't possible when we were in the first year of mourning..." she added hastily, seeing her sister glance at her disapprovingly. "But now you are here, it would be a fine opportunity for you to meet everyone."

"I suppose it would, at that," he agreed.

Caroline clapped her hands and looked delighted and asked, "May I arrange it, then?"

"If it will give you any pleasure, cousin."

As Jonas Ferrar had already concluded, so now Harriet was forced to conclude that Caroline had quickly found the way to manage Stanton. He seemed not to mind anything she said, even her worst gaffes, or being pestered for details of French coiffures, or asked for the sixth time to describe Bonaparte, whom he had seen at close quarters in Vienna, and considered, "A medium fine looking fellow, with a clever kind of face." To this he had added cryptically, "I wouldn't buy a horse from him." For the Grand Army, however, he expressed boundless admiration and did so now.

"It seems to me," said Harriet, goaded, "that an army where any foot-soldier may aspire to be a general must be very ill led."

"Then that is where you are wrong," Ben said. "It is a very ill officered army where a man buys his commission and has no other qualifications for it than a private fortune and an old family name. All the French officers I met with were well trained, intelligent, excellent fellows. I suppose they have their share of rogues, but any army has that. There are old families among them, too. Not every French aristocrat is kicking his heels in exile in London or St. Petersburg."

Harriet felt herself being dragged into another argument, and forced herself to remain silent.

Privately, she was more worried about the Misses Drew. They were so trusting. It would not occur to either of them that the new landlord would deal any more harshly with them than the old one. Somehow, she had to plead their cause, and find some good reason why their rent should remain unchanged. But, just at the moment, she could see no way of approaching Stanton on the matter. As far as he was concerned, they had had a discussion on the subject and it was now closed. All the following day, Harriet mulled over the problem, and eventually decided that the very least she could do was to visit the ladies again and put them on their guard. They would be no less distressed to learn of the financial disaster about to strike them; but forewarned, it would be less of a shock. There was no point in antagonising Stanton again just yet, so she prudently asked Henderson the groom to drive her over to the Misses Drew the following afternoon.

They received her, fussing about her in their usual excitable way. "Only fancy, two visitors in one day!"

"Two?" asked Harriet, taking a seat on a rickety sofa, after an elderly and disgruntled cat had been ejected and Miss Mary had rescued her mending.

"Why, just fancy, Harriet, Mr. Stanton rode by this morning on his round of the estate, and stopped and came in to talk to us."

Harriet froze with a sponge cake in one hand and a cup of weak tea in the other. "He's been here already?" Her heart sank. "What did he say?"

"Such a charming man, and so very handsome. I remember his dear father," said Miss Mary, and fell inexplicably silent.

"He was very obliging," said Miss Drew, with a firm look at her sister. "He thanked us very kindly for the jam, and explained that the potted meat had sadly got lost on the journey home. I was most surprised to hear you had been so careless, Harriet dear, but no matter, for I promised to send another."

"Careless? He said I had been careless?" exclaimed Harriet, nearly choking on the sponge cake and obliged to set down the tea quickly before she spilled it.

"Of course, we had been a little worried..." said Miss Drew.

"About our rent," explained Miss Mary.

"It really is very low for this house, and we were afraid..."

"He might increase it."

Harriet's head was turning from one side to the other as this conversation flew back and forth like a shuttledore.

"But he assured us that we need not worry at all," concluded Miss Drew triumphantly. "Our rent would remain unchanged. He had noticed, he said, that the tiles on the scullery roof had been dislodged—they were, in the recent gales—and he would send someone down immediately to mend them, before the water got in."

"Very like his dear father," said Miss Mary. "He was a very charming boy, if a little wild. We missed him so dreadfully when he went to America." She sighed.

Harriet was not quite sure how to respond, but, as it happened, before she could say anything at all, a loud shout came from outside, and Henderson the groom, who had been waiting with the gig, raced past the window and round to the back of the house.

The three ladies left their tea by mutual accord and ran into the kitchen where Daisy, the maid-of-all-work, was shouting and waving her hands, crying out, "I seen him, I seen him!"

"Stop making so much noise, Daisy! What have you seen?" Miss Drew demanded.

"One of them little devils, them Pardy kids, stealing the washing off my line, under my very nose, but Mr. Henderson has caught him."

Sure enough, Henderson appeared in the doorway, red in the face and grasping by the collar a grimy child of no more than eight or nine.

"Stealing," said Miss Drew to the child, shaking a finger in a mittened hand at him, "is extremely wicked, and you will go to hell if you don't watch out."

The infant responded by kicking Henderson in the shins. Henderson roared and cuffed his prisoner on the ear. The child set up a great screech and burst into tears.

"Oh dear," exclaimed Harriet. "Henderson, do let go of the child, he can't escape. Whatever are we to do?"

"Sir Mortimer is the nearest magistrate," Henderson offered, reluctantly releasing his small charge, who made a bolt for the corner of the room and got behind the kitchen table.

"We can't send such a very young child to gaol!" protested Harriet, knowing very well that the law could and would do just that.

The Misses Drew nodded agreement, since despite a firm belief in hellfire, the idea of a child in Bridewell appalled them.

"Let I take him out the back and give 'un a sound thrashing," offered Henderson wrathfully. "Little horror dang near kicked my shin in!"

"You shall do no such thing, Henderson!" Harriet said sharply. She surveyed the child, who glared defiantly at them all from behind the barricade of the table. He could not be said to be at all an attractive little boy. He was very dirty, and someone had cut his black hair in a very rough and ready manner, so that it bristled all over his head like a hedgehog. He had a pinched little face, and his ears stuck out. There was something about his general physiognomy that clearly bespoke "Pardy". Either the dark complexion and the deepset eyes or the general air of defiance, Harriet could not be sure. "Come out," she wheedled, "and no one will hurt you. What's your name?"

But he had no intention either of giving them his name or of leaving his place of refuge.

The Misses Drew were growing more and more agitated, and Harriet found herself with only one possible course of action. "I shall take the child back to Monkscombe, and see if he will talk to us there."

Henderson made a dive for the table, and after a brief struggle, during which the plate of Daisy's cakes was upset and a cup broken, the child was hauled out. He struggled wildly in the groom's grip, like a small animal, kicking and twisting. As he did so, his ragged shirt became separated from his body.

"Hullo," exclaimed Henderson. "Someone has given him a good hiding already, by the looks of it!" He turned the child round and pulled away the rest of the shirt, so that the ladies could see the marks of a ferocious beating across the child's thin back. "Done with a belt, that."

"That does it!" said Miss Stanton firmly. "Back to Monkscombe!"

Stanton was in the stableyard when they arrived. He watched them descend from the gig in silence, glanced at the child, and then looked interrogatively at Harriet. She explained as briefly as possible.

He gave a grunt, which might have meant anything. Then he turned to Henderson, and said, "Best take the child into the kitchen, Joe, and give him something to eat."

"I didn't know his name was Joe," said Harriet thoughtfully.

"The child's?"

"No, Henderson's. I don't know the child's name. We usually call the servants by their surnames, you know."

"You might," Ben said briefly. "I don't."

They made their way back into the house.

"It was civil of you to call on the Misses Drew," Harriet said a little awkwardly, taking off her hat and gloves. "And—and kind of you to reassure them about the rent."

"They put me in mind of a pair of maiden aunts my mother had," he said reminiscently. "Great bakers of pumpkin pie, and could reel off the names of the kings of Israel quicker'n you'd bat your eye." In a more practical tone, he added, "That house needs some repair. When it's fixed up, I'll think about the rent again."

"Oh." Harriet paused, but was no longer unduly worried by this threat. "What about the child? The law treats children so harshly. He is only a little boy, and has been brought up in the very worst company. They probably sent him out to see what he could steal, and I dare say he would be beaten again if he went home empty-handed."

"All the same," Stanton said, "if we let the child go, that's where he'd run to. Home is home, even if it's a bad one, and taking a child away from his familiar surroundings is a distressing business. No use saying that to any Britisher, I suppose, since they all like to send their children off to school as far away as possible, instead of raising them at home. I'll take the boy back later on, and make it clear that I expect him to be well treated."

"They won't listen to you," Harriet said gloomily.

"They wouldn't listen to *you*, Harriet—I can reinforce my argument with my fists if need be."

She looked a little startled at this, but—as he noted with some wry amusement—she seemed to think it a good idea. They began to talk about the Misses Drew's house repairs, but after a few minutes were summarily interrupted.

There was a crash, the door of the room flew open, and Aaron appeared. In the civilised surroundings of the house, he looked an even wilder character than out of doors, and the red mark of the whiplash was still clearly visible on his cheek. He stood with his hands in his breeches pockets and stared belligerently first at Harriet, then at Stanton. "I've come for the kid," he growled. "Downstairs, they says as they don't let 'un go unless you gives the order. Well, I ain't no tenant of the Monkscombe estate, and you don't give no orders to me, *Mr.* Stanton!"

"I recognise you!" Stanton said slowly. "You nearly caused Miss Stanton to have a serious accident yesterday."

Aaron's dark eyes flickered over Harriet. He leaned back against the door-jamb and said insolently, "I don't mean no harm to Miss Stanton. She knows that. I'm a friend of hers, like."

"You most certainly are not!" stormed Harriet. "Who beat that child so shamelessly? Was it you?"

"I don't know," said Aaron carelessly. "All I know is, I'm taking 'un home."

"Is the child yours?" Stanton asked curtly.

Aaron grinned. "He's one of our Lucy's, that one."

"I dare say," said Harriet bitterly and in a low voice to Stanton, "that any one of them could have fathered him. The Pardys are like that."

"The child was caught thieving," Stanton told him. "We are prepared to overlook that, in view of his age—this time. You can take the child back, under the firm understanding that he is not to be mistreated. I'll check on it—so remember!"

Aaron pushed himself away from the doorframe and lounged into the room. He took his massive hands from his pockets and stood before Stanton with his feet planted apart, running his tongue over his top lip. "I told you," he said hoarsely, "I don't take no Stanton orders. They don't mean nothing to me."

"Really?" Stanton said politely. "Then, possibly, this does!"

There was a sharp crack as his fist met Aaron's jaw. The blow was so quick and so unexpected that Aaron met it with his hands dangling uselessly at his sides. He flew backwards, and landed with a crash on the floor. He was up almost at once, springing to his feet and crouching slightly, in the manner of a born streetfighter. But something in Stanton's attitude and expression made him hesitate. He straightened up and, rubbing his bruised jaw, muttered, "I gets your meaning. Do I get the kid?"

"You remember what I said," Stanton told him softly. "I'll be coming by to check on the child. If you try and make trouble for me, then you can be sure I shall make even more for you."

"Aaron..." Harriet said hesitantly. "Will you take good care of the child, if—if I ask you?"

"Harriet!" Stanton said quickly. "Let me handle this."

But Aaron was grinning broadly. "Why, Miss Stanton, you know I'm always willing to oblige *you*!"

He lurched out of the room, and Ben said angrily, "You'll have nothing to do with that fellow, do you hear me? You most certainly won't encourage him!"

"I didn't encourage him!" she gasped. "I wanted to make sure about the child."

"I already did that. You just keep doing like I told you, Harriet. You keep making out the menus and listing up the laundry. Anything else is my business."

AARON COLLECTED THE CHILD, and set off back to their disreputable dwelling. It was getting late, and light was fading fast. Aaron, who had business by night, was in a hurry to get down to the shore where, with two cousins, he was to sail out and meet a Frenchman bringing in a cargo of brandy and perfume. Among the customers who waited eagerly for it was the magistrate, Sir Mortimer Fish, who, while he had no compunction about sending a man to the assizes for a trial which might end in a hanging or transportation for a relatively minor infringement of the law, regarded his own trading with the enemy, at second-hand *via* the Pardys, with a different eye. Aaron touched the sore spot on his chin where Ben Stanton's fist had struck it, and then the mark on his face left by Harriet. He was accustomed to settling disputes with violence, and did not regard these two attacks in quite the way others might have. He would have been surprised if either Stanton had behaved in any other way.

"Should've been ready for 'un, though," he muttered. "Will be, next time." They were out of sight of the house now. Aaron stopped in the road to grip the boy by his thin shoulders and shake him until his head rattled. "You stupid little tow-rag, what do you mean by getting caught?"

"You let go of me!" roared the child defiantly. "Or I'll go telling Miss Stanton and the gen'leman what you got hid down home!"

"Oh, would you, you little brat?" growled Aaron. Then, with a sudden change of mood typical in one of his temperament and background, he gave an uexpected chuckle and released the child, tousling his spiky hair with a roughly affectionate hand. "Getting late. If you and I wants any supper, best be getting along home."

He climbed over a fence and set off across the fields towards the shore, the child trotting along behind him.

PREPARING TO GO DOWN to dinner that evening, Harriet mulled over the day's events and found herself reassessing her view of her cousin. He still did not behave in any way she would have found correct. On the other hand, his own way was certainly efficient. No one had tackled the Pardys before, face to face. She was rather alarmed at the thought of Ben Stanton riding down to the Pardys' cottages to check on the child. Aaron Pardy on his own, on Monkscombe ground, was one thing; the assembled Pardys on their own ground, quite another. She hoped that he would at least take Henderson and quite possibly one or more of the other brawnier men-servants with him.

Harriet sat with a brush in her hand, staring unseeingly into the mirror. Reluctantly, she had to admit that control of Monkscombe's affairs was hers no longer. Menus and laundry lists were capably taken care of by Mrs. Woods, as Stanton must surely know. In effect, she was left with nothing to do and no say in anything. It was a situation which rankled.

"He cannot run the place by himself, even if he thinks he can," she thought resentfully. "He needs me."

But she did not know how to make him see it. She was painfully aware that she did not have the happy knack of knowing how to behave easily and with confidence in the company of men of her own age. With older men, there was no problem. Jonas Ferrar was a dear friend and she never felt anything but complete ease in his presence. But with younger men she quickly became awkward, saying the wrong thing, or worse, saying nothing at all. Their youthful exuberance made her impatient, and their admiration appeared exaggerated and callow. Small wonder that those suitors who had beat a path to her door in the past had been of a sedate and serious disposition. Small wonder, too, that they had failed to touch her heart.

Her eyes focused on her own reflection. Jonas, bless him, had said she was handsome. She pushed up her brown hair and turned her head first one way, then another. Dressing up and titivating to impress Ben Stanton was a new idea, but perhaps it would do no harm to employ a few of Caroline's tactics. She pulled out an old copy of a *Ladies' Periodical* that lay on a table nearby, and began to turn the pages thoughtfully.

She went down to dinner at long last, feeling a little shy. She had, with great effort, managed to pin up her hair as depicted in the periodical, intertwining it with a great deal of blue ribbon in which was pinned a small gold brooch and a feather. The gown was the most recent she had bought, and therefore the most fashionable, though it was nearly two years old, and dated from before the period of mourning for her father. Still, I do not look hopelessly provincial, she thought, but Ben Stanton had recently been both in Paris and Vienna, and the thought made her nervous. There was nothing worse than a country bumpkin dressed to kill. She had not previously thought of herself as a rustic, but Monkscombe was undoubtedly a long way from the fashion capitals of Europe.

"You look very fine tonight, Harriet!" exclaimed Caroline as she appeared, loudly and clearly within Ben Stanton's hearing. As if that were not bad enough, she turned to their cousin and demanded, "Doesn't Harriet look pretty, cousin Ben?"

He stared at Harriet unsmilingly, and she felt her cheeks burn. Already on her way downstairs she had begun to reconsider whether she had done the right thing. Now she bitterly regretted her temptation to make an incursion into fashion, especially the feather. She twitched at her skirts and shuffled her feet.

"Yes," he said at last, a little brusquely. "Yes, she does." More gallantly, he added, "Well, I have two very handsome cousins."

Dinner proceeded in an awkward silence on Harriet's part. She suspected that Stanton was looking at her from time to time, rather curiously, and she became unusually clumsy, dropping her napkin, and making a great massacre of the fish course.

Caroline, of course, chattered on as usual. "James says they haven't caught the French spy yet, but are sure he's still in the district."

Her use of Captain Murray's Christian name immediately seized Harriet's attention and made her forget her own preoccupation. "When did he say it? And since when do you call him James?"

"I've always called him James; it's his name," said Caroline simply. "He told me when he called this afternoon—while you were out, Harriet, calling on the Misses Drew."

"Who gave Captain Murray permission to call and see you?" Harriet demanded angrily, putting down her knife and fork. "To call by in the line of duty is one thing; to call on you quite another. He had no business. You are not to encourage him, Caro."

"I told him he could call," Stanton said mildly. "He asked my permission, very properly."

"You?" cried Harriet. "You aren't responsible for Caro!"

"Indeed I am, Harriet. I am the head of the house—and it is my house—and I say who may make calls at it. Murray is welcome. He's a sensible fellow. I like him—though I never thought I'd ever say such a thing of a Redcoat!" he added with a smile.

"We shall discuss it later!" said Harriet, glaring at him.

Accordingly, she sought him out later in her father's study, which he had made his own and to which he had retired. It was with mixed feelings that she saw him in possession of what had been her father's sanctum, still filled with his personal possessions and books. Stanton was sitting by the fire, his long legs stretched out in front of him, and apparently deep in thought, so that for a moment she hesitated to disturb him and hovered by the door. The room was quite dark, lit only by a pair of candles and the firelight, and she wondered why he did not ring for more light. She was quite startled when he looked up and invited her, "Come on in, Harriet, and speak your mind."

She took the seat opposite him, on the other side of the hearth. "I've come about Caro. You don't know my sister as I do. She—she's of a very romantic disposition. I don't believe she is in love with James Murray yet, but it could come about if he were to call here regularly. It wouldn't do, not at all. I needn't explain the reasons to you."

"Largely financial, I take it?" he replied. "Or have you a marked objection to scarlet coats?"

"I've no objection to the military at all, but no one, I fancy, thinks them very well paid. That's why an army officer needs an income of his own, besides his pay, if he is to keep up appearances in any way, especially if he is to marry."

"You can't run another person's life for him, or her," Ben said unexpectedly. He leaned back in his chair. It was the winged sort, and the upholstery, the poor light, and the dancing flames all combined to cast a shadow over his face so that although she could hear him, she could not make him out, and it was disconcerting. "Tell me," asked his voice, "why have you seen fit to dress so fine this evening?"

"I knew it was a mistake," said Harriet despondently. "I dare say you think I look ridiculous."

"I didn't say so. As a matter of fact I think you look real pretty. What I don't understand is, why tonight?

You don't usually seem to take much interest in how you look, if you don't mind my saying so.''

"I do mind!" she said bridling. "I hope I'm always decently presentable.''

"You are, and as plain as a Quakeress. Not but what if a woman's handsome, it shows up anyhow. But I like to see a girl turned out nice.''

"Do you?" she said uneasily. She had not given any thought to his private life before. Certainly she had not considered what his relationships with women might be. He was a fine-looking fellow, not short on self-confidence. For all she knew, he might well have left a trail of broken hearts behind all over Europe. Her foot touched against his outstretched ankles, and she withdrew it hastily.

In the darkness, unseen by her, a wry little smile crossed his face. "I don't mean for you and Caroline to go without the things you need, or want," he went on, moving his feet out of the way of hers. "Dresses and ribbons and Cologne water, all that kind of thing. Women like to keep themselves well supplied, I guess. You just order what you want, and I'll pay.''

"I—we—couldn't do that," she said awkwardly. "Though I'm sure you mean it kindly. The money is yours; we don't have any call on it. Nor would it be quite proper, although we're cousins, you know... It would look odd, to other people.''

"Would it?" He sounded faintly depressed. After a moment's silence he went on, "I meant to tell you earlier that I'm going to Bristol tomorrow and shall stay some days, maybe as long as a week. There are details to clear up with Ferrar and I can't expect the old man to come out here. Weather is getting worse—it might even snow. So, if you've any commissions for me—anything you want brought from Bristol and which won't set the neighbourhood gossiping—let me know. I don't mind playing pedlar. Tell Caroline."

"Thank you," Harriet said.

"I've been looking around in here." His hand moved in the shadows, indicating the extent of the room. "Do you happen to know if there's a map of the area anywhere?"

She was startled, and disliked the idea that he had been rummaging in her father's books and papers. A map. She felt a renewal of her old suspicion. "I dare say I could put my hand on one—but why?"

"I thought I'd ride over to Bristol. Don't want to get lost. Got lost once back home, up in the mountains, tracking deer. Snow was on the ground then, and I holed up in a disused cabin. There was a big snowfall overnight, and when I woke up, I opened the door to find just a white wall…snowed in. Had to dig my way out."

Harriet said slowly, "Are you very good at that? Hunting on your own, I mean, tracking animals? It sounds rather difficult and dangerous."

"An old half-breed Indian showed me how. He taught me to read signs. It's real pretty country up there in the Appalachians. Wild. You don't see anyone else for days—weeks, even."

For the first time in her life, Harriet felt a longing to travel and see the world. Twice she had been to London, but otherwise she had journeyed only as far as Bath or Bristol. Now she found herself thinking almost wistfully of all the scenes he must have gazed on, and the variety of people and customs. Monkscombe had been her whole world, and she had never thought she wanted any other—until now. But there was a whole different world out there, and she had seen virtually none of it.

"I believe," she said carefully, "that Philadelphia is a very fine city."

"So it is. But I'm not a great one for cities. What I'd like to do is travel west of the mountains..." A new enthusiasm touched his voice, which she had not heard before, and she peered curiously into the gloom, trying to make out his face. "It's a whole continent, Harriet, and hardly a white man set foot on it, not between the mountains and the west coast where the Spanish hold sway. Nothing but wandering Indian tribes, following the buffalo herds, and may be a trapper or two. There's land for the taking. Miles and miles of it. A man could set himself up there on a piece of earth so big that you could put Monkscombe down in one corner and lose it."

Seriously, Harriet said, "I dare say Monkscombe does not appear much to you, but it has been my whole life. I never went away from it except for visits. I had a season in London, and didn't like it at all. The streets smelled so bad, and everyone was in such a hurry all the time. I couldn't belong there. I belong here. You see, Stantons are Monkscombe," she finished awkwardly.

Ben leaned forward, clasping his hands and resting them on his knees. The movement brought his face out of the shadows, and the firelight flickered on his lean features. Harriet felt a curious stirring inside her, a kind of fluttering. She wriggled on her chair.

"What I told you, the day I came, about my father..." he said, "it was the truth. You didn't believe me, but he always talked about Monkscombe. I think, in his heart, he never left it. He always regretted it. I don't say he wanted to come back, but he couldn't quite make the break. He was an Englishman by birth and he couldn't shake it off. Now me, I'm an American, born in the year of the Declaration of Independence, and proud of it. I can't see Monkscombe with your eyes, but that doesn't mean I don't appreciate it."

He leaned back again into the shadows. "It's a wonderful thing, one family living for so many centuries in one place. Before you came in here tonight, I was sitting here and thinking: my grandfather sat here of an evening, and his father, and his before him. Some of the furniture looks like it was here all that time. Maybe it was. Some of those books up there—" he pointed at the shadowy shelves "—they're almost two hundred years old. When you open them, you can smell the years. Mine is a new country. My mother's family has been settled over a hundred years there. They were Dissenters who left England in Cromwell's time. But they're the exception. Here in England people respect a thing, a family or its name, money even, only if it's old. In America everything is new, and it's no disgrace. A man can wipe the slate clean and start over, right from the beginning, like being born again. What he does on that side of the ocean, not what he's done on this, that's what counts."

She knew then, listening to his voice in the quiet room with only the flickering fire crackling in the background, that they would never keep him with them indefinitely. Sooner or later he would go. She had been of that opinion before, but for different reasons. She had regarded his eventual departure from Monkscombe's point of view, the problem of an absentee landlord. Now, suddenly and to her amazement, she found herself considering it from her own personal viewpoint. She did not know how she felt about it. It was as though he had just opened a door for her, or a window, on to a strange and fascinating land. Not just a land of mountains and rivers and rolling empty plains, but a world of new experience, a land that existed only in the spirit and the heart. Perhaps there were things in that new land, for which she was ill prepared.

Through her thoughts, she heard Ben's voice asking, "I can leave it all with you, then?"

"I'm sorry," she faltered, starting. "I wasn't quite paying attention."

"I said: I can leave Monkscombe in your capable hands while I'm away next week? You'll mind it for me?"

"Oh, yes, of course," Harriet stammered, taken aback at what was rather a reversal of policy on his part. She almost added, "If you think I can manage more than a laundry list!" but managed to stop herself, because obviously he did think so or he would not have asked. She rose to her feet, and said a little nervously, "I think I must be tired. If you don't mind, I'll say goodnight."

He got courteously to his own feet, and said, "Why, you just run along," and then, without any warning, and before she had time to do anything about it, he stooped and kissed her, not on the cheek, which would have been bad enough if just permissible, but on the mouth.

Harriet gasped, and scrambled back, her lips tingling, and put out a hand to ward him off before he tried to repeat his action or did anything worse. "Don't! Don't do that! You shouldn't—you mustn't!"

"Why?" he sounded amused. "Aren't we 'kissing cousins', as they say in the mountains?"

"Oh no!" cried Harriet fervently. "Oh no, we're not. We most certainly are not!" She turned and fled inelegantly from the room.

CHAPTER FOUR

BEN STANTON SET OUT for Bristol so early the following morning that by the time Harriet came downstairs to breakfast, he had already left. Secretly she was relieved. She could not help feeling that she had made rather a fool of herself the evening before. It was only a cousinly kiss, and she had reacted like a startled fawn. He had not meant anything by it, and it was embarrassing to think she had not accepted it with greater sang-froid. But then, she thought sadly, she had not Caroline's happy ability to accept any mark of attention as quite natural and no more than her due. Caroline would not have been thrown completely out of her stride by a simple kiss. Caroline would probably have returned the kiss enthusiastically and bidden him a light-hearted goodnight.

Caroline did not have a very light-hearted appearance this morning, however. Harriet, seeing her sister so listless at the breakfast-table, wondered for a moment if it was on account of Ben's departure, but dismissed this fancy a little uneasily.

"Are you sickening for anything, Caro?" she demanded suspiciously over the coffee-pot.

Caroline stretched her arms above her head and then folded them behind it in an unladylike but expressive gesture. "It seems so dreadfully flat now that cousin Ben has gone off to Bristol, and for at least a week." She pushed back her chair and stuck out her feet in front of her, surveying them. "I mean to arrange our party for as soon as he gets back. Lady Williams had such a nice little orchestra to play for her ball. Perhaps they will come and play here, even though it won't be such a grand affair. We shall be able to waltz, which is all the thing, you know."

"It will cost a great deal of money!" said Harriet firmly. "A couple of fiddles would do as well, and a few sets of country dances. It is cousin Ben's money you propose to spend, Caro, not ours. You should remember that."

"Cousin Ben says I shall have whatever I want," said Caroline obstinately. "He says he will dance with me, and is looking forward to it. He said I should buy a new gown—you too, Harriet."

"I've already gone into the matter of our expenses with our cousin," Harriet told her, "and I've explained that we cannot allow him to meet our dress bills. It wouldn't be right, Caro."

Caroline jumped up in a flurry of petulance. "You are such a spoil-sport! You know you would like a new dress. I know I should! Didn't cousin Ben say how well you looked last night? You always want to make yourself look dowdy, Harriet. I don't know why you do it. If cousin Ben wants to pay for my new frock, I shall let him, so there!"

It was useless talking to Caroline when she was in a mood like this, and Harriet let the matter drop for the time being. There was, in any case, something else she wanted to discuss with Caroline while Ben was safely out of the way.

"About Captain Murray, Caro. He is a very nice young man, but you should not behave so as to hurt his feelings. You know you wouldn't really wish to do that. You should tell him outright that you don't wish him to call any more. In any case, he is not to come here while Ben is away. I think it wouldn't be right.''

"Wouldn't be right, wouldn't be right, wouldn't be right!'' chanted Caroline rudely. "You are a perfect prism, Harriet: you have all the makings of a real old maid! No wonder you spend so much time visiting the Miss Drews. I'm sure you are quite at home there!''

"That is quite enough, Caro!'' Harriet cried angrily, but her sister had already danced away, humming waltz melodies.

Harriet sent down to the stables to have the gig harnessed. When she arrived herself on the portico, ready to take the ribbons, she found, to her displeasure, Henderson waiting to drive her.

"Mr. Stanton said I was to drive you, miss,'' the groom said stolidly when she attempted to dismiss him.

"You know I'm quite able to drive myself, Joe,'' she said crossly. She had taken to calling him "Joe'' since Ben did so, and now it seemed odd ever to have called him anything else.

"That's not for me to say, miss. You'm a tidy little whip, I know—but Mr. Stanton being master here now, his word is what goes.''

Harriet eyed him thoughtfully, then said graciously, "Please help me up, Joe.''

The trusting Henderson handed her up into the gig, but before the groom could jump in himself, Harriet had flicked the chestnut sharply with the reins, the startled beast jumped forward, and the gig bowled down the drive, leaving the stranded Henderson swearing audibly behind her.

She felt a little unkind at tricking the groom in this way, but she had been driving about the estate unaccompanied since she was sixteen, and did not see why one unfortunate accident—or near-accident—which was none of her fault, should make any difference. Henderson was not likely to tell Ben what had happened and admit his own negligence, and what Ben didn't know, did him no harm!

She made her usual round of visits without mishap, and set out for home feeling quite pleased with herself. About a quarter of a mile from the house, just before the gates, when she had already relaxed her hands and allowed the chestnut to take them both home by himself, a figure appeared abruptly in front of her and grasped the bridle.

"Aaron!" she shouted angrily. "We are not going to have this nonsense again!"

"Now don't get into a fret," said Aaron placatingly, coming to the side of the gig. "I ain't going to set the horse off, like happened before. See here, I didn't mean you no harm, as well you knows, and to show I'm sorry, like, as you got a bad fright, I brought you something."

She saw that he held in his hand a small package wrapped in tattered paper. This he thrust into the gig, and stood back with a grin.

"Whatever is it?" she demanded. "Whatever it is, take it away, I don't want any presents from you, Aaron Pardy!"

"'Tis a good present, that one," said Aaron. "'Tis what ladies like—and don't go thinking I don't know what ladies like!" He gave a chuckle of ribald laughter at this, and before she could do anything had set off down the road at a great pace, vaulting over a stile and disappearing across frost-silvered fields.

Harriet picked up the little package gingerly and unwrapped it. It was a small bottle of French perfume...expensive, and smuggled. A part of Aaron's latest cargo.

"Oh, no!" Harriet muttered. She sat with it in her hand, wondering what on earth she could do. She could not just throw it away; someone might find it. But to keep it would be to put her in the position of having accepted a gift from Aaron Pardy, of all people. She put it into the pocket of her pelisse, resolved to return it to him at the first opportunity.

When she got home and made her peace with Henderson, Harriet took the bottle upstairs and hid it in her handkerchief sachet. She did not want Caroline, above all, to find it. Caro, she strongly suspected, would have not the slightest scruple about using it, despite Captain Murray's lectures on the iniquities of smuggling.

BEN ARRIVED HOME at the end of the week. He did not seem to be in a very good mood, and Harriet wondered if he had somehow received bad news. He was preoccupied, and although he had remembered to bring new novels and five yards of Honiton lace for Caroline, as she had begged him, he had little to say about his visit.

A few days after he had returned, however, Harriet was surprised to see him stride briskly into the morning-room where she was sitting. She was engaged in sewing on the new lace for Caroline, who was an impatient and slapdash needlewoman, and had successfully wheedled Harriet into doing the task for her.

"If you're not busy, Harriet, I'd be obliged for a little of your time. There—there are things I need to discuss with you." Ben stood over her, his expression and manner truculent, as if he awaited opposition.

"Why, of course," she said, setting aside her work, and looking at him with slightly puzzled eyes.

He glanced at the abandoned needlework, seemed momentarily side-tracked, and asked, "Is that for you?"

She explained, and he gave a snort of what sounded much like disgust. At any rate, he seemed even more ill at ease and turned restlessly up and down the room, which was unlike his usual easy, assured manner, and convinced her that something must really have gone badly wrong during his visit to Bristol. At last he went to the door, opened it and glanced out to make sure that no servant was lurking and closed it again, turning to face her.

"As you know, Harriet, I've had several meetings with Jonas Ferrar, and he has not spared himself any effort in explaining all the details of the Monkscombe estate, and the entail, to me, and spelling out my responsibilities." He paused, and then muttered, "Yes—responsibilities." He scowled to himself. "Now see here, Harriet, you're a sensible girl and maybe you've already guessed what I'm about to say—or what Jonas said to me."

"No," said Harriet truthfully.

"Confound it, Harriet, you must! Well, never mind." He waved his hand irritably. "Jonas has been explaining your situation to me, yours and Caroline's. I told him you both had a home here at Monkscombe and that there was no question of my turning you out. He seemed to think that wasn't enough. I told him I was prepared to pay your bills, only you seemed to think that inappropriate. The old man got very wheezy at that and sneezed snuff all over me. He said it was a question of a lady's reputation. Cousin or no cousin, I had arrived from the other side of the ocean and was to all intents and purposes a stranger. Your situation, and Caro's, here at Monkscombe, he described as 'nebulous'. At best, he pointed out, it depended on my good will. At worst, people might fancy—well, anyway... I should, he informed me, put things on a proper basis. Seems these sorts of circumstances are not unusual with entailed property... The usual way to arrange things..." Harriet's heart sank, anticipating what he was about to say. "...is by a marriage. I should marry one of you, in other words." He stopped pacing up and down and wheeled round on one booted heel to glare at her aggressively.

"I'm sorry Jonas said that," said Harriet, when she was able to control her shaking voice at all. "He meant well. He's a little old-fashioned, you know."

"No, he's right," Ben said obstinately. "Marriage would make one of you mistress of Monkscombe by right. I couldn't throw you out, even if I wanted. You would feel secure here. There would be no scandal about my paying bills for dresses and folderols of all sorts. Well, that's the way Jonas sees it, and I'm inclined to agree."

He fell silent and threw himself down in a chair, stretching out his long legs and staring at her. He obviously expected some reply. Harriet turned it all over in her mind. Her initial reaction was to reject the whole notion out of hand, but now she forced herself to consider it as a practical proposition. It certainly had happened enough times before, in other families. There was a lot of truth in what he said. The arrangement suggested would be especially beneficial to Caroline.

If he married Caro—Harriet began to warm to the idea—if he married Caroline, her sister's future would be assured. She would continue to live in comfort in the home she had always had. There would be money to pay the many expenses she ran up as a matter of course. Caroline had liked Ben from the first, and moped when he had left for Bristol. On his side, Ben seemed to be taken with his pretty young cousin. He was happy to indulge her whims, run her errands and let her fill the house with musicians and dancers. An engagement between Caro and Ben would deal neatly with the looming problem of James Murray. Harriet was sorry for James, but he would get over it, and it was by far the best thing. James could not keep Caroline in the style to which she was accustomed. Ben could.

Harriet straightened her shoulders, and said more brightly, "Well, I should be very happy to know Caro is settled. I'm sure she would make a very good wife and mistress of Monkscombe. She may seem a little giddy, but that's only because she is very young, and she really is quite sensible underneath it all."

Amazement entered the grey eyes watching her. "Caroline? And what am I to do with the lovesick Redcoat? Call him out and fight a duel?"

"I'm sure Captain Murray will understand that it is in Caro's best interests," Harriet said confidently.

"Are you, by jiminy? I should think he is more likely to come haring round here and punch me on the jaw! Besides, I'm most thirty years old, not a boy who has only just learned how to hold a shaving-brush. I can do without a nineteen-year-old bride whose head is full of novels, dancing partners and new dresses. I want someone who can run Monkscombe for me when I'm not here. As you have done this past week. No, I mean that I should marry *you*, Harriet."

She turned as white as a ghost, and he thought for one moment that she was about to faint. He said irritably, "Well, I might not be the ideal bridgegroom of your dreams, but I didn't think the prospect would appear that bad."

Harriet said in a stifled voice that sounded quite unlike her own, "I am, you know, only fit to make up menus and laundry lists. Suppose you have to leave me for more than a week?"

He sighed. "Don't sulk, Harriet. You've more sense than that. I was only joking—well, not entirely, not at first. I wanted to see how capable you were before I left you in charge of the shop."

"Shop?" she shrieked, causing him to start in alarm. "Monkscombe isn't a shop! And have you the effrontery to tell me that I have been *on trial*? Do you realise I have been running Monkscombe for more than a year, since Papa died and while we all waited for you!"

Ben gestured soothingly at her. "For pity's sake, woman, haven't you got an ounce of humour in you?"

"I have an excellent sense of humour, thank you!" said Harriet tartly. "You have a very poor sense of when it is a suitable time to make jokes."

Ben jumped to his feet. "I am not joking, confound it, woman! I am making you a proposal of marriage. I am not Murray, though, and I do not have the slightest intention of crawling about the carpet on my knees! However, you have known Jonas a good many years, and I should have thought you respected his judgment even if, as it seems, you have such a poor opinion of mine!''

''Jonas said I should accept you?'' she whispered, dismayed.

''Yes, he did. He said you have your head screwed on the right way, and would see the sense in it.''

Harriet began to feel the walls of the room close about her. She was boxed in. They had already decided it, between them. Jonas, with the best of intentions, had betrayed her. ''Oh, but I...'' she stammered. ''I hadn't thought about it. I am twenty-six, you know, and had—had rather put marriage out of my mind. There was always Caro, you see, so much prettier, and—and more able to chatter away to men in the way they like. I—I am all right in practical matters, but not much good at—at anything else.''

Something of Ben's irritable manner evaporated. He lost the look of dogged embarrassment, and stooped over her in his usual more assured fashion. ''See here, Harriet, it's a peculiar sort of a situation for both of us. But I don't mind telling you I should be very pleased to have you agree. You're a fine-looking girl, and have a good brain, and why, I'd be really proud to have people say: There goes Mrs. Ben Stanton!'' He smiled down at her.

''Instead of there goes Miss Stanton!'' she said wryly, and they both laughed.

Ben slapped his hands on his knees cheerfully, and, to her further consternation, reached out and pinched her cheek in a familiar caress. ''There you are. Things should work out pretty well, you'll see.''

Harriet's sense of claustrophobia increased. Surprise, and finding herself in a totally strange situation, had deprived her of her self-possession, and he obviously assumed, in the absence of a vehement refusal, that she agreed. She opened her mouth and stammered, "Oh, but I didn't mean..." The words dried in her throat as her previous idea of securing Caro's future, recurred to her. It might still be done. "If I were mistress of Monkscombe, Caro could stay here and have all the things she wants. Neither of us would have to go away, ever, and it would be our home as it always was!" she thought.

Ben had straightened up and turned away. Apparently, he had not heard her last unfinished phrase. "Now, unless you can think of any good reason why we shouldn't, I'll make the announcement at that dancing party Caroline is so set on arranging. Get the neighbours together, and send 'em away with something to gossip about when they get home again!" He swung round on his heel and stared down at her again.

"It would do that," said Harriet, thinking of Sir Mortimer, Lady Williams, the rector, the Misses Drew and all the rest of local society. "It would set the whole neighbourhood by the ears." Now, or never. Refuse—or allow him to presume that she agreed. She had to make a decision.

"I'll do it!" she thought. A sudden qualm struck her, as she looked up at his tall form towering over her. But things would not be as they had been before. There would be more to being Ben's wife than being mistress of Monkscombe. There were those other wifely duties he would expect, and to which he was entitled. She hoped he would be a little understanding about that, and not too disappointed if she did not turn out to be the most satisfying of mistresses in that other sense. She bit her lip and watched him move towards the door.

"Oh," he said, turning back as if he had just remembered. "Jonas said he'd be happy to give you away, if that suits you."

Harriet said, "Oh—yes..." and saw that he looked relieved at having got the whole thing over without any female hysterics or serious objections on her part. He gave her a parting smile and nod, and went out.

THEY AGREED THAT no mention of the engagement should be made before Caroline's party. Especially, said Ben firmly, not to Caroline herself.

"Telling Caro, and asking her to keep it a secret, would be rather the same as giving a message to Paul Revere and asking him to pass it on," he observed.

"Oh, yes," said Harriet quickly, "She does prattle, rather."

Privately, she was more than pleased that no one else should know, not just yet. Any delay was welcome. But her situation with regard to Ben was, in many ways, worse than it had been before.

Most lovers, as she well knew, tended to hold hands and whisper in corners, whenever they could do so unobserved. They exchanged meaningful glances. They wrote sentimental letters, and filled their pockets with keepsakes.

She, however, existed in a no-man's-land. She was indeed engaged, unofficially and secretly but nevertheless engaged, to marry him. She could not cry off. Well, she could, but a lady did not do that sort of thing. She felt, therefore, an obligation to look pleased whenever he came into view, and to appear to enjoy his conversation and his company. The truth was that, despite some reservations, she had begun to enjoy his company, but quite paradoxically, would have enjoyed it more without the nagging secret of their betrothal. She was frightened to smile at him, lest she appear to simper and look smug. She shied away from any familiarity, in case he took it as an invitation to start some kind of lovemaking. She had a terror of finding herself alone with him, and found as many excuses as she could for going out of the house altogether.

On the days when she was not suffering these agonies, she suffered another kind of torment. This marriage was not Ben's idea, it was Jonas Ferrar's. Ben had agreed, out of duty. She, Harriet, if she could not look enthusiastic, should at least look grateful. But this notion caused the old fires of resentment to flare up in her heart. Grateful! Grateful, for being given the opportunity to live in what had always been her home, and which had been taken from her by an unjust quirk of the law? In fact, she thought fiercely, she was not being given the opportunity at all, she was buying it—buying it with her hand in marriage. It was a sordid, mean little bargain, viewed in that light, and she was ashamed of it.

Ben took her silence and her obvious avoiding of him fairly well, to all appearances, and went off to visit the Pardys to check on Harriet's youthful protégé. He took Joe Henderson with him.

"The Pardys," said Joe heavily, as master and groom trotted over the heathland towards the shore and the Pardy cottages, "is a thorough bad lot. You won't think me speaking out of turn, sir, if I says we ought not to go down to the house. Call it a house!"

he added in some disgust. "'Tis more like a pigsty. Blessed if I can see how folks can live like it."

"I want to see the child, Joe," Ben said firmly.

"Then we stay by the gate, and we shouts to them to send the kid out."

"We are obliged to, anyway, Joe. The Pardys' house is their own, and we should be trespassing if we were to force our way uninvited past their gate," Ben returned mildly.

The mild tone did not deceive Henderson, who grinned.

As it turned out, "gate" was an optimistic description of the entrance to the pair of dilapidated cottages that housed the Pardys and, apparently, their livestock, all under one crooked roof. There was a sort of fencing about the place, but what had once been a garden about the two cottages was now only a sea of mud, trampled and littered with every kind of refuse. The way the Pardys dealt with anything unwanted was, it seemed, simply to throw it out of the door. Where it landed, there it stayed until the weather or the pigs took care of it. As Ben and Henderson drew rein, an ugly lop-eared cur with matted fur ran out and snarled at them, snapping at the horses' heels, until Henderson reached out and aimed a blow at it with his riding-crop. The dog retreated and growled at them from a safe distance.

At the doorway appeared a young woman, clad in a dirty gown and with lank, uncombed hair. As soon as she saw them she ran back into the cottage.

A few moments later Aaron stepped out of the door and stood there with his thumbs in the armholes of his waistcoat, surveying them. Behind him loomed a second, and even more unprepossessing, figure with broad, hunched shoulders and long, swinging arms.

"Good God, who or what is that?" exclaimed Ben.

"That'll be Nathan Pardy," Henderson explained. "I do know that one, and a bad sort he is. Always into brawls, and a dirty fighter, if you know what I mean. Been took up before the magistrate more than once— but the magistrate being old Sir Mortimer, he has always got off."

"What does that mean?" Ben asked sharply.

Henderson shifted his seat in the saddle slightly. "Why, sir, Sir Mortimer being a fine old gentleman, he likes a glass of brandy."

And the Pardys obligingly smuggle it in for him, thought Ben drily. So the fine old English gentleman is open to corruption.

From the door, Aaron called out, "What brings you, Mr. Stanton?" He grinned.

"I want to see the child!" Ben called back.

"And supposing, like, we refuses? Will you come fighting your way in here, with Joe Henderson there behind you?"

Behind Aaron, his cousin Nathan burst into laughter. Henderson muttered an oath.

"Stay here, Joe," Ben ordered quietly. He rode forward, pushing open the rickety contrivance which passed for a gate. The dog barked once, and then scrabbled back out of the way, to crouch, waiting. As Ben rode up to the door, both Pardys stepped out of it to forestall him.

"The child, Aaron," Ben said gently.

Aaron surveyed him thoughtfully. "See here, Mr. Stanton—you notes I'm polite, I hope? I ain't no friend of yours, but I am a friend of Miss Stanton's."

He saw that this brought an angry flush to the other's face, and his own grin grew broader. "So, just to oblige Miss Stanton—and I hope you'll tell her so—I'll let you see our Billy. Fetch the kid out, Nathan."

Nathan disappeared, and returned dragging the child, wriggling and protesting, by one arm.

"Let him go!" Ben ordered. He leaned down in the saddle and called, "Come here, Billy."

The child was unwilling to respond, but did so when propelled forward by an ungentle shove from Aaron.

"Are you well, Billy?" Ben asked him. "Speak up. No one has been hurting you?"

Billy mumbled indistinctly, but was interpreted as saying he was all right. He then turned and bolted back into the house.

"Now I hopes you're satisfied, Mr. Stanton," said Aaron, "and we won't be having the pleasure of your company no more."

"That depends!" Ben said curtly. He turned and rode back to the gate.

Watching the two riders clatter away, the Pardy cousins exchanged glances.

"May have to take care of him," Nathan said judiciously.

"Oh, don't you worry," his cousin assured him. "The gentleman maybe has his weak spot, after all, and I fancy I knows what it is." He chuckled.

BEN AND THE GROOM rode homeward, but when they were still some way from the house they came upon the main road from the village. As they approached it from one direction, Ben's sharp eyes spotted a female figure walking briskly along a footpath towards it from another.

"You go on, Joe," Ben said slowly. "I don't need you any more."

Henderson glanced towards the approaching female form. "Very good, sir," he said blandly, and set off at a fine pace.

Harriet, stepping out energetically as a way of combating the cold, sighed when she saw the waiting figure on horseback ahead of her. She reached the stile and clambered over it unaided, although he swung down from the saddle to help her.

"Now then," he asked, surveying her, "where have you been?"

She was panting slightly from her walk, and her hair was untidy. Her hat had slipped and was stuck on the back of her head in a jaunty manner. She had pinned up her petticoats to avoid the mud, but revealed a pair of very trim ankles. As she scrambled over the stile, she revealed rather more by way of very shapely legs.

"I have been to the rector to fetch his sick list," she said, "and from there to see one of the shepherds, whose wife is lying in."

"Sick list?" he queried. "Is that necessary?"

"Yes. You see the rector, as a bachelor, has some little difficulty with visiting all the sick, especially women who are lying in, so I do it."

"I see." He frowned, and slapped the reins against his thigh. "When you say you visit the sick, I take it you don't go running round houses where there is fever?"

"Dr. Gray does that. Although I have been, on occasion, to make sure that they were doing as Dr. Gray told them. Hanging up wet cloths, to make sure contagious miasma does not escape from the sick-room, and so on."

"I see, I don't know that I care for that—however," he added hastily, seeing the familiar mutinous glint apear in her eyes, "I, too, have been about good works, as you will be very pleased to hear. I went to see the Pardys—about the child."

"You didn't go alone?" Harriet cried in alarm.

"Why, no, I took Joe Henderson, who is built like a brick barn and well able, I'm sure, to take care of himself. But I'm flattered that you were worried about me."

"There is no flattery in it," she told him crushingly. "I was worried because the Pardys really are dangerous, and quite capable of wreaking mischief by way of revenge. Did you see the child?" she added.

"Yes, he seems well enough. Although a child hardly belongs in such squalor." He turned the horse's head towards home, and they began to walk along the road side by side. "The wind has sprung up and is carrying rain on it, unless I'm much mistaken," he observed. "It might be a good idea if I took you up behind me, and we got home that much quicker."

"I don't mind a little rain. Ride on, by all means, if you wish," Harriet said hastily.

"And leave you to trudge after me afoot like an Indian squaw? I know you don't think me a gentleman, but even primitive fellows like myself don't abandon ladies in such circumstances. Here..." He paused by a fallen treetrunk at the roadside. "This is as handy a mounting-block as any. Jump up."

"Oh no, I can't!" wailed Harriet in dismay. "Someone might see us, and think it very peculiar!"

"They would think it more peculiar to see us both walk in the rain when we are provided with a horse."

He stopped and swung up into the saddle. "Come along."

Harriet climbed unsteadily on to the log and held out her arms. He leaned forward, and pulled her easily up on the horse, so that she perched behind him.

"Are you ready?" he asked over his shoulder.

The horse set off. The first movement almost set Harriet back on the ground again, and she threw out her arms in fright and clasped Ben tightly round his waist. It was as well she could not see his face or she would have seen that he was laughing silently to himself. They progressed in this fashion for half a mile, and then the heavens opened and a real downpour broke over their heads. Ben reined up and jumped down from the saddle. He reached up and dragged her down beside him, and they both ran through the lashing rain for the shelter of a nearby outbuilding. It was empty, and not in very good repair, but at least it kept off the worst of the rain. Ben led the horse inside and tethered it. Then he turned to see what Harriet was doing, and saw her shaking her skirts disconsolately.

"What you need when you go visiting, Miss Stanton, is a good large umbrella. Anyway, I don't know why you had to walk in this weather."

"You took Henderson," she said crossly. "And I am not allowed to drive myself, if you recall."

"Hmm." He took off his hat and shook it, sending a spray of raindrops through the air. "Well, perhaps the weather has done us a favour, after all. We can sit here, as it is fairly dry, and talk cosily until it clears up."

"Talk cosily?" she asked with bated breath, moving away from him and staring at him with huge eyes. "What about?"

"Well, we are an engaged couple, so we shall discuss our wedding plans. I am not for making a great fuss about weddings myself."

"Neither am I," said Harriet with more enthusiasm than was quite necessary.

He had found a disused crate and dragged it forward, dusting it off with his handkerchief. He sat down, and indicated that she should join him. She did so unhappily. There was not much room, and they were squashed together in the sort of proximity she was not accustomed to where men were concerned. To her absolute horror and dismay, he took hold of her hand.

"I shall, of course, buy a new coat. Blue, they tell me, is the thing. Shall you have a white dress, Harriet?"

"Yes," she said gloomily. "But I shall pay for it myself, because it would be a nonsense if you paid for it."

"What a stickler you are for the proprieties," he said with a sigh. "In my free and easy transatlantic way, I couldn't give a fig who paid for it."

Harriet took her hand from his. "I think, cousin Benjamin, I am beginning to recognise your sense of humour. I know very well that you are making fun of me. I suppose you don't mean any harm, and only want to tease me, but I don't like it and I wish you wouldn't."

There was a silence, broken only by the patter of the rain on the roof. Ben said soberly, "I'm sorry. I had no wish to upset you."

He made no attempt to repossess her hand, but his thigh rested against hers, and there was no room on the box to move along out of the way.

"I have been thinking," Harriet said in a desperate little voice, "about marrying you ..."

"You can change your mind; it's a lady's prerogative." His voice was expressionless, but he watched her averted profile closely.

"No." She shook her head firmly. "It's something no lady should do. I wouldn't dream of breaking the engagement. I shall, of course, marry you, if you insist. But I would appreciate it very much if *you* would release me from our agreement."

This time the silence was longer. Ben got up and walked away from her a little, his hands behind his back. Suddenly he whirled round and struck out ferociously with his riding-crop at a nearby pile of sacks. Grit flew into the air, and a rat, disturbed by the action, scuttled out. It had hardly appeared when Ben stamped hard down on its head, and then kicked the carcass out of the way. During all this he had said nothing, but the violent gesture with the whip and the ruthless elimination of the animal were so expressive of some pent-up emotion that he dared not put into words that it froze the marrow in her bones and deprived her of any further speech. He turned round, and stared at her. His face might have been carved out of stone.

"Why did you agree when I first suggested it?"

"To—make sure of a home for Caro and myself at Monkscombe," she faltered.

"Then nothing has changed." He moved towards her, but seeing her shrink as though she were afraid of him, stopped. "That was the reason for my offer, and those circumstances are the same now as then. You may think I made my offer lightly, but I most certainly did not. I am not accustomed to have my generosity turned down, Harriet. No, I will not release you. Break the engagement, if you wish. *I* do not break it."

"I have told you that I cannot break it," she whispered. "No lady does such a thing."

"Then we shall be married, Harriet," he said brusquely, "and there's an end to it." He walked to the door of the barn and peered out. "I do believe the rain is lessening. I'll set you up in the saddle, and lead the horse."

She muttered, "Yes, of course..." and this was how they finished their journey home, and in silence.

NOT SURPRISINGLY, Harriet slept very badly that night. Very late, she had no idea at what time, she awoke with a feeling of unease she could not quite explain, even in the circumstances. She felt in the darkness for the candle and tinderbox, and managed to strike a light.

The candleflame sent irregular shadows leaping round her room. They had frightened her as a child, but not now, because she knew the house so well, and it was a friend. She always felt that nothing bad could happen to her here. Or at least she had always believed so, until now.

She got out of bed and went out into the corridor. It was empty. She turned, and was about to go back into bed, when she heard a distinct creak from the floor above. Someone was awake, and walking about—up there. For an instant her blood chilled, all the old ghost stories suddenly real. But she shook herself and told herself that it was only one of the maids who slept in the attics. The footsteps above her head creaked again. She crept to the stair at the end of the corridor, and clutching the candle and her night-gown to avoid tripping over it, cautiously ascended.

In theory, no one slept on the floor above. There were some rooms, but they were small and inconvenient. There was also the door that gave access to the Widow's Walk. As her head drew level with the top of the stair, she felt a draught of cold night air. The door to the Widow's Walk stood open. It should have been locked. It was inconceivable that it could have blown open without the hand of man! She crept cautiously along the corridor to the door, set down her candle, lest it betray her, and felt her way along to the opening.

Suddenly Harriet found herself staring at the night sky. The door to the Widow's Walk gaped open wide, and outlined against the stars was the tall silhouette of a man who stood outside on the gallery and looked towards the sea. He was watching something by the moonlight with the aid of a spyglass. She held her breath, then quietly withdrew, collected her candle and retreated cautiously downstairs to her own room.

There she lay awake until morning, seeking in her mind some possible explanation to account for Ben's keeping a lonely and secret night vigil, watching—for what?

CHAPTER FIVE

CAROLINE THREW HERSELF heart and soul into arranging her party, and displayed an ability to dragoon others that surprised Harriet. The orchestra was arranged, the guest-list was drawn up and invitations written out and despatched. Mrs. Woods was consulted about the food, and elaborate arrangements were made to make vast quantities of soup which, in the current cold weather, should keep without spoiling until needed. The doors connecting the main drawing-room and the dining-room were thrown open to make a larger area for dancing, the dining-table and chairs were removed, and every maid in the house set to polishing the parquet.

The family, in the shape of Ben, Harriet and Caroline, was obliged to dine in a small back morning-room which was hardly ever used, was dark and gloomy, and filled already with unwanted furniture.

"It's very inconvenient, Caro," Harriet protested mildly, but was overwhelmed.

"Don't fuss, Harriet dear! It's only for a little while, and I'm sure Ben doesn't mind. He hasn't said so."

Perhaps Ben had also been taken aback by Caroline's unexpected fervour and might well have wondered what demon he had unwittingly unleashed. As for local society, that promised to come in droves. No one had expected much entertainment before Christmas, and an extra party at the beginning of December was greeted with surprise and delight, especially by the younger members of the community. Privately, Harriet wondered where they would put everyone, since only a few people lived near enough to return home the same night, and most would want lodging. This meant, in addition to everything else, turning out bedrooms, hunting out linen and the feverish counting of plates and cups. To Harriet fell the task of allotting bedrooms and deciding who might share. Caroline was concerned with choosing the music. Ben went down to the stables, and stayed there.

But Caroline's enthusiasm went beyond mere practical arrangements. She descended on her sister with a gleam in her eye, and a determined manner. "Now, Harriet, I will not let you come down dressed in any old gown and looking a perfect fright."

"Thank you very much, Caro. I never thought myself a perfect fright."

Caroline continued, unabashed. "There isn't time to have new gowns made, it's a shame. I shall wear my ivory silk. Let's see, what do you have?" The door of Harriet's wardrobe was pulled open and one by one her gowns appeared and were tossed unceremoniously on the bed. Eventually Caroline emerged backwards, hair disarranged, flushed and triumphant, holding up before her a pink taffeta with rose velvet ribbons.

"Oh no," said Harriet quickly. "Not that one. I never liked that one. It was a mistake. It's much too elaborate for me."

"Nonsense, Harriet. Come and try it on so that we can see if it needs any alteration."

Harriet stood in front of the bedroom fire, and patiently allowed herself to be pulled, pinched and manipulated in all directions, before Caroline declared the dress a very good fit, and the very thing, if only Harriet would do her hair nicely. "As you did the other evening, when Ben liked it so much."

Caroline sat on the edge of the bed amid the welter of discarded gowns, oblivious of the chaos she had created. "I do so want this party to be a success," she said earnestly. "I feel it is a very important occasion."

Harriet darted a suspicious glance at her. Surely Caroline could not have guessed what a momentous announcement was to be made on the occasion of her ball? But Caroline's expression was one of dreamy anticipation.

"By the way," asked Harriet, "have you sent an invitation to Captain Murray?"

"Oh yes," said Caroline absently, "of course I have." Her expression altered slightly to become less complacent. "To be sure, I've seen very little of James lately. He is all the time riding about the countryside looking for that Frenchman. He is so convinced that the man is hiding around here somewhere. Honestly, James talks about nothing else!"

A petulant note entered her voice. Harriet pursed her lips and grew thoughtful. It was most annoying, but when Captain Murray had been all attention, Caroline had not been too much concerned about him. Now that his attention was elsewhere, her interest seemed to have been piqued. Harriet hoped the gallant Captain would prove to be a poor dancer. In the current state of affairs, that would do him no good at all, in Caroline's eyes.

"I wish," said Caroline unexpectedly, "that James was able to resign his commission in the militia and were not so dependent on his pay. But he has two elder brothers, you know, and there isn't a chance he will become the heir. I can't think it agreeable to be married to a man who is always worrying about his duty. Not that I don't admire James, and I'm sure he's very brave. But his conversation is all muskets and saddles, if you know what I mean."

Harriet did not know whether to be encouraged or dismayed by this speech, and put her trust in the Machiavellian hope that the Captain would prove to have two left feet.

Anyway, she had worries nearer to home than Caro and James Murray. Within the week, her engagement to her cousin would be known to all. Ben would be unlikely to want to delay very much before the actual wedding. Harriet paused in gathering up the gowns Caro had left scattered about the room and glowered at her bed. She imagined herself lying in it, which was not difficult or alarming. She imagined Ben lying in it, which was disturbing. She imagined both of them in it together—and the prospect was so terrifying that she felt an impulse to run away altogether and never come back.

It was not in her nature, however, to give in to circumstances. The night of the ball arrived, and Harriet went upstairs and prepared her toilette to the best of her ability. Despite herself, she found herself feeling quite pleased with the result. In a house full of ladies in ballgowns, the pink taffeta did not look so outrageous, but quite in place. Her hair stayed up very well with the aid of no fewer than twenty-three pins, and her mother's pearl earrings, which had come to

her as the elder daughter, looked very nice. She thrust
her fingers into her handkerchief sachet for a suitable
lace-trimmed wisp of material, and they closed on
something hard. She withdrew her hand, and found
herself looking down at Aaron's bottle of French perfume, lying on her open palm.

She had forgotten all about it, with so many other
things to take her attention. Now she unstoppered it
and sniffed cautiously. It was unquestionably the real
thing, and very expensive. Perhaps Aaron, in his
rough way, was sincerely sorry for the fright he had
caused her, and the gift was genuinely meant. Even so,
it had to be returned. However... Harriet took the top
off the bottle again... However, a very little would not
be missed. She could dab just a drop behind her ears,
and the bottle would still look untouched. No one but
herself would know that it came from Aaron's bottle.
More than one lady here tonight would wear French
perfume that had been obtained just as illegally. She
owed it to Ben, thought Harriet, to make the best of
herself—in view of the momentous announcement he
was to make. She dabbed a little of the perfume
quickly behind her ears, re-stoppered the bottle and
thrust it away again in the sachet. There, no one would
be the wiser.

Thus prepared, she went downstairs to make a last
check of all arrangements. The house was already full
of people, and maids were running about all over the
place with crimping-irons and needles and thread, as
the usual last-minute panics took place. Sir Mortimer
Fish was already asleep in the morning-room, to which
he had prudently retired. At his elbow stood a bottle
and a glass. Against the glass was propped a note,
which read, "Wake at suppertime."

Harriet went back into the hall as a blast of cold air announced a new arrival and found herself facing Captain Murray, who was stamping his boots and announcing gloomily that it looked like snow. She welcomed him, and he confided, "This isn't my sort of thing at all, Miss Stanton. Caroline says I am to waltz. Well, I've tried it, and I can't get the hang of it. Anyway, it don't seem quite decent to me, taking hold of ladies like that, not in public," he added with disarming candour.

"Never mind, Captain, do your best!" said Harriet kindly, patting him encouragingly on the arm.

Ben was invisible, but a maid, scurrying past with Lady Williams's shawl, said that the master was in the library. Like Sir Mortimer, Ben was hiding. But he ought to be greeting his guests. With the intention of recalling him to his duty, Harriet tapped on the door, and opened it.

He was standing at the far end of the room, leaning on the mantelshelf and staring down into the fire. He glanced round as Harriet came in, and straightened up. His tall, muscular frame looked very dashing. She stood by the door, and fiddled with the handle, suddenly shy.

"Oh, Harriet," he said with some relief, "there you are. Who are all these people? Caroline's still upstairs, and not a soul is around to introduce us. I refuse to stand out there and welcome people I don't know."

Harriet's courage returned. "It's all right; we'll go out and welcome them together, and I can tell you who they all are."

He came closer and surveyed her somewhat moodily. "You look beautiful," he said simply and soberly.

"Oh..." Harriet wriggled in the gown. "Thank you. It is mostly Caro's doing, you know."

"I was just thinking over our discussion of the other day, in the barn. I am a little hasty-tempered, I know, and I didn't mean to seem brusque."

Harriet looked down. "That is all right. I do understand. It's a very kind offer you've made, and it was very rude of me to try and back out of it. It was just that I..." She paused, and tried to think how she could explain it to Ben. But she couldn't, there were just no words.

"You had cold feet," he said, with a slight smile.

"No, I wasn't cold," said Harriet. "It wasn't that."

He burst into laughter, and then said, "No, you noodle! I meant you had taken fright... at having committed yourself."

"Yes," she said uneasily.

"And does the idea still frighten you?" he asked, quite seriously.

She wanted to say, Yes, it terrifies me... but she only mumbled, "I've quite got used to it now, thank you."

"I thought, perhaps at supper," Ben said. She stared at him a little blankly, and he added, "I could announce it, at supper."

Harriet swallowed. "Yes, that's—a very good idea."

He smiled, bowed and offered her his arm. "Then let us go out and do what's required of a good host and hostess."

Harriet returned the smile a little tremulously, but suddenly her heart felt much lighter. She began to think how silly she had been to be so frightened about the whole thing, and that perhaps, after all, being married to Ben would be really rather nice...

He saw the tense expression fade from her face. When she did not look as worried as she frequently did whenever he hove into view, she really was a beauty, he thought. And frightened out of her wits. He wished there was something he could do to reassure her, but she had some very fixed notions where he was concerned. He was a stranger, and he would stay a stranger. But she was a very lovely girl, the candlelight lent intimacy to the room, and they were alone together. In the far distance, muffled by the door, came the sounds of the orchestra tuning its fiddles vigorously. And because it seemed the most natural thing in the world to do, he stooped and kissed her.

He thought she might fly out of the room in a panic, as she had done before, but this time she stood her ground and only looked up at him so wonderingly and timidly, unsure what to do about it, that his own heart gave a disturbing little lurch. He thought, Oh, darnation...because the whole thing was not as simple and tidy as that wily old fox, Jonas Ferrar, had described it when he had been talking Ben into it. Ben was fast beginning to wish that, when he had received the lawyer's letters informing him of his inheritance, he had simply written back and said he did not want it. He should never have come near Monkscombe. He should have stayed away and minded his other business, and left the sisters to live in the place without the inconvenience of his company.

He said, a little awkwardly, because he felt awkward, like a tongue-tied boy, "That is French perfume, unless I'm much mistaken."

She started and he thought she blushed, although he could not be sure in the dusky candlelight. She muttered, "Yes, but only very little."

"It's difficult to get nowadays in England, or so I should have thought," he commented, but then he thought, However, Sir Mortimer gets his brandy, and perhaps this perfume arrived in the same way. He frowned, because he did not like to think that Harriet dealt in smuggled goods. It seemed so out of character for her to do so. She was the most honest and upright of persons. He asked, with genuine curiosity, "How did you come by it?"

"Someone gave it to me," Harriet mumbled.

He raised his eyebrows. "Recently, then. It doesn't stay fresh indefinitely." An unwarranted touch of jealously struck him. "Who?" he asked, more sharply.

A less honest person would have lied to him. Afterwards, he recognised that. All she needed to say was "Lady Williams", or some such person. He would have accepted it, and enquired no further, because it would have been highly indiscreet to ask how or where Lady Williams had acquired it. But she was honest, and took a deep breath, like a child about to confess some horrendous infant sin.

"Aaron did."

Ben caught his breath. At first he felt rather as though someone had hurled a bucket of cold water over him, and then his temper, which he had already admitted occasionally got the better of him, sent a flame of searing hot anger racing through his veins. In a low, hard voice, he said, "Pardy? That—that ruffian?"

"I meant to give it back!" She stumbled over the words and stared up at him with huge, frightened eyes. "Only I haven't seen him again."

Ben removed his arm from hers. "You mean, he quite literally *gave* the perfume to you? You didn't buy it?"

"No, it was a present. You see, I met him when I was driving..."

"You were driving?" he interrupted her harshly. "I told you that Joe was to drive you if you wanted to go out."

"I know, and it isn't Joe's fault, don't blame him, please. I played a sort of trick on him. It was underhand, and I shouldn't have done it, because he trusted me. But I've always driven..."

"I said you were not to do it!" he roared at her, so that she feared he could be heard beyond the library door. "I don't give a damn what you did before. This is what you do now! You do not drive round the countryside unescorted, and you do not, by thunder, accept gifts from Aaron Pardy!"

She did not lack courage, and she was not accustomed to be shouted at. A militant sparkle entered her eyes, and she ceased to be apologetic. "I do not accept gifts from Aaron, or anyone else!"

"You certainly don't from me!" he said cuttingly. "I'm not allowed to pay for a few yards of material, lest it cause a scandal. Smuggled perfume from one of the neighbourhood's most notorious ne'er-do-wells is, however, apparently a different matter. You have a curious notion of decency! I might call it hypocritical."

Harriet stamped her foot in fury. "I don't take presents from Aaron!"

"You took that one!"

"He surprised me. He threw it into the gig, and ran off. It's not my fault!"

"It's your fault you kept it!" Ben thundered, getting more and more angry, and doubly so, because he could not control his own fury. His long hair fell over his face and he began to pace up and down, gesticulating wildly.

"How was I supposed to return it? Walk down to the Pardy cottages?" she hurled at him.

"No, damn it, you should have sent Joe Henderson down there, or waited until I got back and given it to me to return!"

"I didn't want you to know!" she yelled, and then fell silent, appalled at this admission, which, while true, was ambiguous.

"Oh, did you not?" he said coldly. "I can imagine so. Well, let me make this absolutely clear, once and for all time. Until we are married, and more especially after we are married, you will have nothing more to do with Aaron Pardy. You will not encourage him. You will accept nothing from him, and ask nothing of him. You will not even meet with him. Is that understood?"

"I have lived in this part of the country all my life, and so has Aaron," she panted. "I don't like Aaron, I don't like the Pardys, I don't want to see Aaron, and I don't want his gifts, but I will not be told whom I may meet and who not—and Aaron for all his faults at least belongs here, and you don't!"

She had never said anything in her life which she wanted more to take back as soon as the words had left her lips. But it was too late, and she could do nothing to rectify her error. How could I have said it? she bewailed her action in her head, and watched Ben with bated breath.

He ordered tersely, "Go and get it."

"What?" she whispered.

"The perfume, confound it! Go and bring it here—*now*!"

In the face of such complete anger, the more frightening because he no longer shouted but held himself in icy control, Harriet could do nothing but retreat obediently to the bedroom, retrieve the perfume bottle and take it back to the library. She handed it to Ben with a slightly shaking hand.

If he noticed the tremble, he did not show it. He took the bottle and thrust it into his pocket.

"What will you do?" she ventured to ask.

"Return it, of course, tomorrow—as tonight is inconvenient."

He smoothed back his hair and straightened his cuffs. "Now take my arm, and we'll show ourselves to our guests."

I HOPE I NEVER have to experience another evening like this one, Harriet kept thinking. To emerge on Ben's arm, looking self-possessed and cheerful, was a feat worthy of a medal. To chatter to people about this and that, to keep an eye on the supper arrangements and do a dozen other things called for a clear head and ordered mind, which she sadly lacked at the moment. As supper-time approached, her inward disarray grew greater. Would he still make the announcement? He probably would. People would crowd round to congratulate her. She would be required to look happy. She feared that it was beyond her.

Then she glanced at Ben, and thought with some compassion that it was as bad for him. He was still angry, but he had not to show it. He had to make the announcement as though he considered himself the most fortunate man in the world. He probably considered himself the unluckiest. Obstinacy alone sustained him. He had said he was going to marry her; he *would* marry her.

She, on her side, had agreed. She could not escape. Harriet glanced at the longcase clock and sent a footman to wake Sir Mortimer for supper.

The announcement, when it came, was received with all the cries of surprise and delight that she had imagined. Sir Mortimer, after the news had been twice shouted into his ear, actually hobbled across, kissed her hand and promised to dance at her wedding, which—as he had not danced a step that evening or (as he informed her) since Christmas 1792—raised alarming possibilities. Lady Williams expressed benign approval, and regretfully shelved the plan with which she had been toying and which involved her youngest daughter Lavinia, whom her mama would have been happy to see the lady of Monkscombe. Caroline gave a great shriek, rushed down the room and embraced her sister heartily. "I knew it! I knew it! And it is so romantic!"

Harriet prayed that the floor might open up, or the roof fall in, but neither of these happened. Supper was cleared. The orchestra took its place and struck up, and she was obliged to allow her fiancé to lead her on to the floor. She moved in a fog of bright lights, chattering voices and smiling faces. The faces came and went, peering closely into hers, and mouthing at her words she could not hear. She was aware of nothing but teeth. Good teeth, bad teeth, gold teeth, false teeth. They all grimaced at her in well-meaning congratulation.

Amid it all, Ben's face appeared and her eyes focused on it, bending over her. His voice asked, from a million miles away, "Would you like to sit down?"

"Yes, please," she mumbled, and he led her to the side of the room. Someone put a glass of negus into her hand. Caroline appeared, perched alongside her, and fanned her energetically with an ostrich-feather fan borrowed from Lady Williams.

"There," said Caro happily. "I said my little party would prove a very important occasion!"

EVEN WHEN HARRIET FINALLY gained her bed, utterly exhausted, in the early hours of the morning, she was to have no respite. Caroline had given up her own room to the Williams girls and shared her sister's bed. She chattered brightly until nearly dawn, although her sister buried her head in a pillow and answered not a word.

Both finally fell asleep as light crept over the landscape around the house. Harriet opened her eyes towards noon. It was very quiet. Caroline slumbered on beside her. There was not a sound anywhere. The light in the room seemed strangely luminous, and there was a cotton-wool feeling about it all. Harriet scrambled out of bed and ran barefoot to the window.

Overnight, it had snowed. Not heavily, and with luck it would not prevent any of their overnight guests from leaving. But everything looked fresh and white, a new world, untouched and untroubled. She sat on the window-seat, shivering in her nightgown and contemplating the scene. Suddenly she heard the thud of hoofbeats from outside, and leaning forward, saw Ben appear on horseback and set off at a smart trot towards the gates. He was going to return the perfume. She sat back, and wondered when she had last felt so miserable and the future had looked so bleak.

BEN RODE ACROSS a deserted winter landscape. The horse's hoofs sank into the soft thin crust of snow with a dull, muffled thud. Other creatures had been out and about before him. Narrow, straight holes through the snow marked the earlier passage of a fox, and everywhere were the triple clawmarks of birds. Of man there was little, if any, sign. As a youngster, he had sat and listened spellbound to hear his father talk about this place. Ben could remember every story: of the great seamen-adventurers who had sailed from the ports of the West; the tales of smugglers and wreckers; of Monmouth's great rising and its dreadful defeat, followed by the bloody passage of Judge Jeffreys through the West Country, when every crossroad was marked with a gibbet and a swinging corpse and the grisly remains of men hung, drawn and quartered were hung up in salutary warning in marketplaces and on village greens. Of William of Orange's more successful attempt, marching victorious through the West towards London and a crown. Highwaymen had frequented these lonely hills and moors. They had passed into legend. In reality, they had probably been uneducated ruffians much like Aaron Pardy, but memory lent them an aura of gallantry and romantic association. Aaron and his kin were direct descendants of those men. They carried on their traditional business; contraband. Harriet had been quite right to say that Aaron belonged here and that he, Ben, did not.

It was not Ben's country, and it could never be, yet he felt the pull of its fascination. Especially today, when he could not fail to be aware of how wild, desolate, windswept and ancient it was. Caesar's legions had marched across these hills. Before them the Celtic tribes had held their secret, savage rituals here. The power of their sinister, magical, powerful deities was still imprinted on the landscape. There were odd stones, strange hummocks, curious earthworks. Who knew their significance? Written history is but an insignificant fraction of all that has gone before. Aaron, in his own way, represented that darker side of the West Country. Ben would always be a stranger here.

Aaron Pardy. Ben scowled. In the clear light of day, and with his anger stilled, he knew it was inconceivable that Harriet should entertain any liking for that rogue. Yet stranger things had happened. Aaron liked to boast of his amorous conquests, and according to Joe Henderson, it was not mere boasting. Local girls, it seemed, fell in droves for Aaron's brutish charms. But he aspired higher. Aaron had turned his eyes towards Miss Stanton of Monkscombe. Why? The challenge? A twisted sense of humour? The desire to be revenged on a society that outlawed and scorned him while secretly making use of his services? The envy of the have-not for the haves? Or even a genuine attraction?

Why not? thought Ben. Harriet Stanton, beautiful, spirited, well dressed and well educated, must compare with the sluttish, unwashed, illiterate drabs of Aaron's acquaintance as a coursing greyhound compares with a tinker's mongrel cur. Ben did not reckon Aaron's interest in Harriet to be of no acount. It mattered. It mattered more, probably, than Harriet herself realised. She, it was painfully obvious, knew little or nothing about their physical natures and the potential ferocity of their physical desires. Harriet thought she could take care of any problem presented by Aaron. Ben knew she could not.

He tapped his hand against his coat pocket and felt the hard shape of the perfume bottle. Confound his impudence! How dared he? Ben fumed silently. Did the scoundrel really think that, sooner or later, he would achieve what he wanted? Ben had no doubt what that was. Oh, yes. Aaron had conceit and confidence enough to believe that he would—in one way or another. Harriet, on her encounters with Aaron when she went out alone, ran a risk she probably did not dream possible. That Aaron might carry force against her as far as that had not crossed her mind.

"But you have reckoned with me, Aaron Pardy," Ben murmured grimly to himself, aloud.

The difficulty was to explain the reality of the situation to Harriet in a way that would not make her more terrified of men than she already was, but which she would accept. So far, apart from shouting at her and ordering her not to go out alone—an order she consistently disobeyed—he had not found the way to do it.

He was riding now along the line of a low cliff above the shore. He had already marked this spot from the Widow's Walk at Monkscombe. On a clear day, and with the aid of his spyglass, he had noted the fishing-smack at anchor off the little bay. Now he drew rein and rested his hands on the pommel of the saddle. The wind tugged at his hat and blew chill around his ears. The horse lowered its head miserably and moved to turn its broad backside into the blast. Down below, on the beach, the fishing-boat had been pulled up ashore and was propped up on blocks of wood to allow maintenance work to be done on her. She was large for a fishing-boat. But then, she did little fishing: she carried other cargo. Three men were working on her down there, even in this cold weather . The boat had to be seaworthy. Her cargo was valuable.

Ben took up the reins and kicked his heels into the horse's flanks. A little further along the cliff he came to a steep path cut in the side of it and leading down to the shore. It was narrow, and the covering of snow made it slippery, but it was also very well maintained. Up this path were carried the casks of brandy and other goods to be loaded by night on to the waiting line of pack ponies on the cliff top. Ben had marked that, too, from the Widow's Walk. He had sat up there by night, and seen the flickering lights of torches. He supposed a good citizen would have reported it to the excisemen, or at the very least to James Murray, but Ben was wary. He was a foreigner and an outsider. Sir Mortimer was probably not the only local magistrate to be hand in glove with the smugglers. Ben would be seen as an interfering nuisance, and steps might well be taken to eliminate him. He felt faintly sorry for James Murray, who was an honest fellow and trying his hardest. But Murray had more stacked against him than a band of illiterate smugglers. The Captain was chasing will-o'-the-wisps!

Ben urged the horse down the steep incline. Its hoofs slithered and stones rolled away, falling on the beach below. The men working there must know of his approach, but they took no notice, only carrying on with their work. He could hear the tap of their hammers and the scrape of their boots as they climbed over the boat's sides. When he was a few feet from the bottom, the horse leapt off the path and landed on the beach. Ben was almost unseated, and reflected wryly that it was best to concentrate on the immediate matter in hand. The men were waiting for him. They would not go away. He rode towards them, and some twenty feet away drew rein and sat motionless.

He recognised Aaron, and Nathan, but did not know the third man. However, he was probably kin of the Pardys. No one took heed of him for a few minutes, and then Aaron left his work and came slowly towards him. He stopped a few feet away and eyed Ben insolently. He still held in his hand the hammer with which he had been working. That might have been chance, but most probably was not. Behind Aaron, the other two men had not stopped working, but they worked more slowly, and their eyes watched.

"Well, Mr. Stanton," said Aaron. "And what do you want this time? Seems you've a powerful strong liking for visiting me."

"My business is with you alone, Aaron," Ben said, loudly enough for the other two to hear. He put his hand in his pocket and withdrew the perfume bottle. "Here, catch!"

He tossed it towards the other as he spoke, and automatically Aaron threw up his hand and caught the little bottle. He glanced down at it, and an ugly expression crossed his face. He looked up at Ben, but before he could speak, Ben cut in, "You'll make no more gifts to my future wife, is that understood?"

Surprise touched Aaron's coarsely handsome features. Then he smiled mockingly, and said, "Oh, that's the way of it, is it?"

"That's the way of it," Ben said curtly. "You'll stay clear of Miss Stanton, and you'll put out of your head any notion you might have there. You won't even bid her good-day, Pardy."

He pulled the horse's head round, and because it would be twice as difficult to get up the slippery incline as it had been to come down, he rode off along the shore, to where he knew there was an easier way some half a mile distant.

Aaron stood watching the disappearing figure of his opponent. "Oh, we'll see about that, Mr. Stanton," he said softly. "We maybe knows a trick or two hereabouts that you don't."

CHAPTER SIX

ODDLY ENOUGH, now that the news of their engagement was known to all and sundry, Harriet found the idea easier to accept in her own mind. She had thought that the opposite would be true, and that the feeling of being trapped would increase. But just not having to keep the engagement secret any longer was a relief. Caroline, of course, tended to prattle on about how romantic it was, and how she had guessed from the first and all kinds of nonsense. James Murray had also come to congratulate Harriet with unfeigned fevour, gripping her hand in a clasp that crushed her fingers and obviously hoping that once Miss Stanton was safely wed, the way would be open for Miss Caroline to tread the same path to the alter—with luck, with him.

One way and another, it was impossible, not to like James. It would be easy, she thought, to get very fond of him and to welcome him happily into their family circle. His influence on Caroline was to the good, he supplied the sense she sometimes lacked, and although head over heels in love, had no compunction about lecturing her firmly on her faults. But aside from his modest militia pay he was quite penniless, and the prospects of promotion in the county very poor. He had even begun to talk of trying to get himself transferred to a regiment of the line. It would not be difficult in these troubled times, and his country would doubtless be more than happy to have him. For some time, Britain's war against the French had been conducted at sea, and with success. Only the previous October had come news of the notable naval victory in the Bay of Trafalgar, which had both exhilarated the nation and plunged it into despair, as the price had been the loss of its hero, Admiral Nelson. But in Europe itself, the tale was different. The Grand Army rolled inexorably onward, and the allied forces seemed powerless to halt its progress. The armies of the European powers in disarray, Britain saw herself drawn nearer and nearer to the day when British forces would have to be deployed in a continental war. Already the recruiting sergeant had become a familiar figure in scattered villages.

That James might take up a regular commission filled Harriet with panic. Life in garrison towns was makeshift and uncomfortable, the company very mixed and often coarse. There would be sights and sounds undreamed of by Caro, who had led a sheltered life at Monkscombe and would be ill prepared for the hurly-burly of garrison life and the intrigues and quarrels of army wives, or the drinking and gambling of the regular officers. Even worse, if a British force were sent to some European field of operations and James went with it, the prospect for her was grim indeed. Wives did accompany their husbands on campaign, but it was hardly desirable. Harriet could not imagine Caroline facing the rigours of an army on foreign soil, sleeping in a tent, eating food cooked over campfires, setting up home in squalid billets surrounded by outlandish peasantry whose tongue she could not speak, and risking all the horrors of disease, squalor and starvation.

Her fears for her sister eventually even led her to seek Ben's help, albeit tentatively. She still did not think he was well qualified to give advice about Caroline, but he was a man, and he might talk to James as man to man. James would be more likely to listen.

Ben hunched his shoulders as he listened to her involved explanation of just why it would be impossible for Caroline to follow the drum.

"Murray is trustworthy and honest. I guess he would try to look after Caroline well enough, if it came to that. Other women manage. She's young and fit and healthy. She'd make out."

"She's a gently-nurtured girl!" burst out Harrriet, agitated by his seemingly careless tone. "I knew it would be no use talking to you. I should have known you wouldn't understand."

"Then why did you talk to me, Harriet?" he returned coolly, his grey eyes meeting her flushed gaze with composure.

"Because I thought, as you are on good terms with Captain Murray and he seems to respect you, that if you said it wouldn't do, he'd listen. But there, I see I've wasted my time!" She turned away crossly, in a swirl of skirts.

Ben was distracted enough to consider she had very pretty ankles, but reluctantly wrenched his mind from this interesting detail. "As a matter of fact, dear cousin, I happen to agree with you that really it wouldn't do."

She was surprised. She darted forward and peered up into his face eagerly. "You'll talk to James?"

"I already have done so. I've told him I consider him a most suitable candidate for Caro's hand, which he is—I doubt you'll find a better. But his circumstances leave a lot to be desired, and he knows it himself. He loves Caroline. He'd give her the world, if he had it in his pocket. But he hasn't. So, being a highly practical fellow, he can offer only what is within his province—life as an officer's lady, with all that it means."

"Do you mean to say," she whispered, appalled, "That he has already asked you if he may marry Caroline?"

"In a manner of speaking. Don't worry, I won't let him carry Caroline off to become a camp-follower, with everything she possesses loaded on the back of a mule." He glanced quizzically at Harriet. "Could *you* do that, do you think?"

"I don't know," she said honestly. "I suppose if it meant following the man I loved, I would." She then blushed furiously, and began to talk feverishly about other matters.

Ben was now taking an interest in the estate, and working very hard, so that Harriet began to regard him with a reluctant admiration. He rode miles around the farms, he enquired into everything and was difficult to deceive, and the tenants, she knew, had quickly come to respect him. Perhaps the awareness that he was accepted by local people had eroded some of the defensiveness which had previously resulted in obstinacy and aggressiveness when he was crossed. He was certainly more relaxed and happier. Sometimes, when he met her eye by chance, he would give her a little smile, which never failed to make her heart give a peculiar little hop. Lately, she had taken to smiling back.

That was all very well, as far as it went. But she still avoided being alone with him, because she still did not know what she would do if he took things any further than an exchange of smiles. He had kissed her in the past. Sooner or later he would do so again, and next time, he might expect her to respond.

Christmas approached, and bundles of holly arrived at the house to be strung from the ceilings in prickly green garlands. Joe Henderson carried an armful into the library, and breathed heavily. "Where do 'ee want I to put all this?"

"I'm not quite sure, Joe," said Harriet, staring thoughtfully about her.

"It'd be a mercy," grumbled Joe, "if'n you'd make up your mind sharpish—begging your pardon—only 'tis sticking into me in all kinds o' places."

Harriet begged him to set down his burden while she deliberated. He did so, and departed to fetch a second lot, moving carefully across the floor in his stockinged feet, as his dirty boots had been left at the kitchen door.

Left alone, Harriet picked out a fine red-berried specimen and clambered cautiously on to a pair of library steps. It was not so easy to secure the holly as she had imagined. She began to think she should wait until the groom returned. She made a last effort to reach up to the spot she aimed for, and teetered insecurely. As the library steps rocked, she heard the door open behind her. Thinking it was Joe returning, she twisted round to speak to him, and that was her undoing.

The steps slipped away and overturned with a crash that reverberated throughout the room. Harriet screamed, and plunged backwards into space, saved in the nick of time by Ben, who had thrown himself across the room. He caught her in his arms, but off balance, staggered back and was unable to steady himself without dropping her, so they both landed entangled in a heap on the floor.

For a few seconds, the breath was knocked out of them. Then, panic at finding herself in Ben's embrace, erased any pain from her fall, and she gasped, "Let go of me, I'm all right!" She turned her head as she spoke, and found herself looking directly into his grey eyes. There was something written in them which was new and subtly alarming. A tingle ran along her spine.

He said softly, and a little huskily, "You don't have any call to be scared of me, Harriet. Do you think I'd hurt you?"

"No—no," she admitted. His face was so close that she could mark the tiny weather lines in the tanned skin. She fixed her gaze on his mouth, and something about that made her feel even more nervous. When she had listened to the rector preach on the Temptations of the Flesh, the phrase had seemed no more than biblical oratory. Now it took on a meaning she had never before suspected.

He stretched out his hand and touched her cheek. His fingertips felt damp with perspiration, for all the day was so cold. He could feel her trembling in his arms, like a nervous colt, shying away from the scent and touch of man and fearing his mastery. He whispered, "It's all right, Harriet," and stooped over her. She gave a convulsive shudder, and its effect on him was to destroy his own carefully maintained restraint.

Ben grasped her shoulders, trapping her beneath him, his mouth closed possessively over hers, and though she struggled and pounded on his back with her clenched fist, he ignored her puny efforts. She had never imagined herself in a situation like it. Her heart pounded like a drum, but along with fear, she felt a kind of exhilaration. He had kissed her before, but not like this. No one had ever kissed her like this! She felt herself begin to relax in his arms, and even more incredibly, her body began to mould itself to his. Suddenly, she thought in amazement and dismay, But what am I doing? and knew that things had to stop here, now, or they would reach a point where nothing could stop the inevitable. Fear of that inevitable, and an awareness of something in the way he held her that had been absent before—a roughness, a touch which demanded, not asked, and became increasingly impatient—froze her body.

Ben released her, pushing himself away, and sat up on the floor, looking at her a little strangely. Harriet scrambled on to her hands and knees and scurried away from him.

"I've been thinking," he said slowly, pushing back his unruly long hair and resting his arms on his bent knees, "that I should ride down to see the rector and put up the banns. There is no reason why we should wait at all before being married." His expression was cool and watchful, waiting for her reply. He had regained the control he had temporarily lost, but a wariness, which lately had been absent, was back in his eyes.

"Oh, no!" gasped Harriet, brandishing a piece of holly at him, as if she would ward off both him and the suggestion.

"Why not?" His grey eyes met hers with that look she recognised so well, both challenging and obstinate.

"Because—because it's almost Christmas." Harried plunged into a recital of their Christmas rituals. The festival was such a busy time, she pointed out. Every house of any standing in the neighbourhood gave a party, and local society set out on a month-long pilgrimage that took it from one house to another, successively eating one host out of house and home, before moving on like a band of cheerful locusts to the next. The organisation involved was enormous. In the kitchens of Monkscombe they had already started baking, having hardly got the aftermath of Caroline's party out of the way. So much work for the servants...

She pleaded in vain. The servants were not involved, objected Ben. The wedding would be very small and private, attended only by Jonas Ferrar, who would drive out especially from Bristol to give away the bride and would stay over Christmas, Caroline, and—Ben informed her, perhaps not unexpectedly— Captain Murray.

"Groomsman," he said. "Why should the bride have all the support while I am left standing there with no one? Murray has been very obliging about it. I told him I would do as much for him one day."

If Ben's intention had been to elicit some spirited response to this thinly veiled reference to Caroline's future, he failed. Harriet gesticulated wildly with the holly, and protested, "It's so soon, and there is so much to do..."

In her agitation, she stabbed her hand with the holly prickles and exclaimed in pain. He said, "Let me see

that", and took hold of her hand, turning it over so
that he could see spots of scarlet on the white palm. He
took out his handkerchief and bound it round to stem
the bleeding.

"Harriet, I do believe you do these things to rile me!
You ride round in gigs drawn by horses liable to bolt,
walk miles alone over the fields and clamber over the
furniture. You need a husband, or someone to look
after you. It seems to me that the sooner I ride down
and speak to the preacher, the better."

She realised, staring at him wide-eyed and clutching her injured hand, that he meant it.

BEN RODE DOWN to see the rector the next morning,
and the first of the banns were read out the following
Sunday. After that, the days slipped past. The local
seamstress came and stitched the wedding dress, cop-
ied from the *Ladies' Periodical*. Harriet herself
stitched on the lace, and even Caroline sat and
hemmed seams, singing happily and thinking, perhaps, of her own wedding gown. Captain Murray was
much back in favour. It did not matter, it seemed, that
he could not dance. It mattered more that he had no
money, but Caroline did not trouble herself unduly
even about that, trusting that matters financial would
sort themselves out somehow, even if it meant a regular commission for James and living in lodgings,
about which she—being totally ignorant—entertained the most optimistic and unrealistic notions.
However, Harriet no longer had the will to say anything to discourage her young sister. After all, she had
hardly arranged matters very successfully for herself,
and perhaps she ought not to meddle in Caroline's
plans.

Ben had not to see the wedding gown, of course, lest it bring ill-luck, so they worked away upstairs in Harriet's room, which meant that she saw little of him. One morning, however, he stopped her as she would have left the breakfast-table, and said, "I want to go over to Home Farm, and thought, as the roads are clear and not too badly cut up, that you might drive me in that gig of yours."

She was surprised, but agreed readily. Sitting indoors day after day and peering at tiny stitches was tiring work and she would be glad to be out of doors. She had not driven for some time, either, and would be glad to have the ribbons in her hands again.

"You don't mind," she asked, as they set off, "sitting up beside me and having me drive?"

"No, should I?"

"Some men would, I dare say. Driving is a man's accomplishment, and it is something to be thought a Corinthian."

"You are talking of idle young gentlemen," Ben said. "I am not idle, not a youngster and no gentleman, as you have pointed out."

Harriet flushed. The gig bounced over a stone, and she covered her confusion by calling to the horse.

His business at the farm did not take long. As they were driving home, and had just topped a slight rise, he suddenly said, "Stop here." Harriet drew rein and looked at him expectantly. He pointed ahead towards the distant view of the house, visible from the rise. "Monkscombe, Harriet. Take a good look at it. In a few days from now you will be its mistress. I want you to be sure that that is what you want."

"But of course I do," she exclaimed, surprised, and wondering if it was to ask this that he had brought her out here.

He gave her a somewhat bleak smile. "And nothing else?"

She hesitated. Something inside her seemed to be telling her that there was something else, but she could not be sure what it was, and so could not put it into words. She glanced at Ben, and found herself thinking, I wish things were different. I wish there was not this horrid business of the entail. I wish Ben had asked me to come driving simply because he wanted to be with me, and not because he wanted to know my feelings about Monkscombe. I wish—I wish he really liked me for myself, and that the idea to marry me came from his own head, and not Jonas's, just as James wants to marry Caroline. She remembered that last kiss, and shivered, although she was warmly wrapped up in her fur pelisse. He might not particularly have wanted to marry her, but he was a young, healthy male with all the normal instincts, and he seemed to think that sufficient to justify the intention. As far as she could tell, he entertained none of the obstacles in his mind that plagued her own thinking.

She knew he was looking at her and waiting for her reply. Lacking the words, she shook her head.

"Well," he said, "that's settled, then." His voice sounded flat and expressionless, as if he had ironed out the last detail of a business contract. Perhaps he had. He reached out and took the ribbons from her hands. "Here, let me take us home. I can handle a horse in harness pretty well myself."

They would not discuss it again before they emerged from the little medieval village church on Christmas

Eve, declared by the Church to be man and wife. They were greeted by the Misses Drew, armed with handfuls of rice, and a choir of local children singing "Sweet Lass of Richmond Hill", which Miss Mary Drew had considered a suitable choice of music.

The wedding breakfast passed off well enough. Sir Mortimer drove over, drank the bride's health with a gusto that belied his years, and afterwards settled down in the library to talk legal business with Jonas Ferrar. Caroline disappeared into the music-room with James Murray. After an unsuccessful attempt at a duet, in which the Captain's contribution consisted of the same two chords played over and over in the bass, silence fell over the music-room, though anyone listening at the door, which fortunately no one was, might have heard a certain amount of whispering and laughter. As for the bride and groom, it was assumed that they wanted no company but each other's, and they were left contemplating one another across the drawing-room.

In addition to the Christmas holly, Caroline had insisted on pinning up mistletoe over the door, but so far this tempting garland had been ignored by everyone except Captain Murray, who had eyed it a little wistfully all evening. Harriet sat by the fire in her wedding gown and waited for Ben to speak.

He seemed to be waiting for her. At last, when she showed no sign of saying a word, he observed, "I thought the rector managed very well, and the children sang nicely."

"Miss Mary meant it for a surprise," said Harriet hollowly.

The light had already faded, and they were interrupted at this juncture by the arrival of the candles.

When the servant had gone, Ben got up and, going to the sideboard, poured out two glasses from the wine which stood there. He brought them across and handed one to her. "We should drink a toast to our future—at least, before Sir Mortimer drains the cellar dry."

Harriet smiled wanly, took the glass and did her best not to spill any. She could manage to drink only half of it, however, and sat clasping the rest. Ben put his empty glass on the mantelshelf.

"It's getting late. I'm going to make my rounds. I shall have to go down to the stables. Everyone seems to have Christmas fever in the servants' hall, and although I've every confidence in Joe, I've less in some of his underlings. I dare say you are tired, Harriet. You should go on up to bed."

The wine left in her glass swirled around the sides. Harriet put the glass down, and muttered, "Yes, of course. Shall you . . . Shall you . . ."

"Shall I be coming to join you there? No, Harriet, I shall not."

His tone was crisp and cool, and quite decided. She gave a little gasp, and stared up at him, astonished.

He raised his eyebrows. "You look startled. You thought I would?"

"Well—yes . . ." she stammered. "I mean, it's usual . . ."

"Harriet," Ben said gently, "you have what you wanted. I'm far from certain I have what I wanted. You wanted Monkscombe. You wanted to be its mistress. You are its mistress. I am equally sure that you do not want *me*. You have never wanted me here. You have made it clear to me, over and over again, that I do not belong here."

"I'm so sorry I said that!" Harriet burst out. "I never meant..."

He was shaking his head, his long hair falling forward over his brow. "No, you're right. I don't say it wasn't kind of unpleasant to have you say it, but that doesn't make it less accurate. Of course I don't belong here. However could I? But it doesn't matter, as I shall not be staying indefinitely. Perhaps a year. Then I shall go back to Philadelphia."

"What about me?" she whispered, aghast.

"You'll stay here and run Monkscombe," he said simply. "I told you I needed a wife who could do that. You'll do it very well. You've done it before."

This dreadful, unforeseen twist of events was entirely of her doing and Harriet was horrified at what she had done. The truth was, she had been so wrapped up in her own problems and the difficulties of her situation and Caroline's, that she had given no thought to Ben's feelings. Looking back, she could see that from the start she had been extremely disagreeable towards him. She had started by trying to have him arrested, and when that had been sorted out, had singularly failed to welcome him to his ancestral home. She had poured scorn on his ignorance of their ways, and the needs of an estate, instead of tactfully pointing out how things were managed. She had told him bluntly that her reason for accepting his offer of marriage was a purely practical and selfish one. Now she was faced with the result of all this. He had done his duty. He had made her mistress of Monkscombe. As far as he was concerned, he had done all he needed to do.

"Ben," she said hesitantly, "I really am very sorry for having been so—unfriendly. It was only, you know, being so worried about the estate, and not knowing anything about you . . .''

"Knowing nothing," he pointed out, "you might have kept an open mind, and not just assumed the worst.''

Harriet twisted her hands nervously. The fire spat out sparks from the logs. One landed near her skirts, and Ben stubbed it out with his toe. "You are right to be angry with me," she stumbled on, "but I wish you would let me try to explain, and perhaps even find it in your heart to be a little forgiving.''

She glanced up at him entreatingly as she spoke, but there was little in his face to encourage her. He turned his head away, and kicked at the log in the hearth. Desperation took hold of her. She had mishandled it all so badly, and now she had not the slightest notion how to go about putting matters right. What would Caroline do? Why, jump up and put her arms round Ben and wheedle him into forgiving her. But Harriet could not do that, nor did he expect it. He would probably be horrified if she even tried!

"But I don't want Monkscombe at all," she burst out at last, wildly. "Not in this way. This is not how I wished to be mistress of Monkscombe. Why, it would be quite dishonorable to accept the title and not—not earn it. When I said I'd marry you, I really meant—I really meant to be a proper wife, or try to be a proper wife. I dare say I might not be a very good wife, I mean, you would probably be disappointed in me in— when we were together, but I might learn, if you would be patient, and I most certainly would try!''

"Don't talk such nonsense, Harriet!" he said sharply. He had moved away from the firelight and the candle glow, and she could not see his face. "What kind of man do you think I am? I don't go around forcing my attention on girls who don't want me. Nor, thank you very much, do I fancy going off to bed with someone who looks upon the whole business as a sort of sacrificial ordeal! To act out a kind of charade, in which we pretended to dote on one another and, even worse, to act out some kind of charade in bed—would be just plain stupid! There are certain situations, Harriet, in which it is no use pretending—and that is most certainly one of them!''

For a moment, some of her old resolve returned to her. ''It wouldn't be stupid at all. If I can at least try, why can't you?''

He whirled round and shouted angrily, ''Because no one can build a house without foundations! There is nothing between us to build on, Harriet! A man does know what effect he has on a woman! I do see you run away every time I come into a room. I do feel you freeze when I touch you. I fully realise you don't trust me. You talk so easily about 'trying', but I don't believe you have it in you to succeed, even if you did try! You're a beautiful, clever and capable girl without an ounce of sentiment in you anywhere. You despise it when you see it in others. You treat James Murray's feelings for Caroline as trivial. You say he will 'get over it'. Well, he will not, Harriet, because he loves her! But you, that is something you are quite unable to understand!''

He was shouting, now, so loudly that the glass on the shelf rang. He seemed to realise it, broke off and made a visible effort to pull himself together. ''I am going to check the horses,'' he said curtly.

"Check the horses?" she cried wildly, jumping to her feet. "You not only reject me, you wish to make a fool of me! How will it look to others?"

"It is a matter that concerns only you and me," Ben snapped. "I shall not discuss it with anyone else. You may do as you wish. You pretty well always do so, anyway. Incidentally, I remind you to stay clear of Pardy. In the public eye, you will be recognised as my wife—and my wife, like Caesar's, must be seen to be above suspicion!"

"You insult me . . ." she breathed in a low, shaking voice.

"Well, then, it is one insult returned for the many I've received from you," was the terse reply. "Goodnight, Harriet."

He walked quickly to the door, and it slammed behind him. Harriet was in such turmoil that she hardly knew what to do. She could feel the tears stinging at her eyelids, but was determined not to cry. Being rejected is, nevertheless, one of the most demoralising of experiences, and her emotions ricocheted between despair and wounded pride, so that she hardly knew what she felt. On the one hand, she felt like running after Ben and shouting out loud, for all to hear, that she didn't need him, didn't want him, and could manage, thank you, very well without him. Then she thought, no one must know! It would be too humiliating. Harriet Stanton, rejected on her wedding night and told to her face that she was cold-hearted, calculating and not the sort of woman he wanted in his bed! From this, she fell back into despair again, and bewailed her own stupidity and lack of experience. Every little maidservant had her sweetheart, but Harriet Stanton turned into a tongue-tied idiot whenever she found herself alone with a man, freezing in his arms, and unable to hold his attention even on their wedding night.

A slam of a distant door, and the shrill chatter of Caroline's voice stilled her confusion and brought her to a sense of the moment at hand. They were coming—they must not find her! She couldn't face them. Not only could she not bear to have them witness her humiliation, she could not bear to see their happiness in each other. Harriet leapt to her feet, ran from the room and up the staircase, to barricade herself in the safety of her own bedroom. There, at last, she took off her wedding finery, clambered into the bed that had been made up with snowy white lace-trimmed linen, a bridal bed, and curled up in a dejected huddle to sob her heart out in the pillows.

BEN RAN DOWNSTAIRS to the stableyard, knowing full well that he had probably left his bride of a few hours behind him in tears. It was not, he told himself angrily, his fault. He had never wanted to inherit the wretched place. He was hardly to blame that his uncle had failed to father a son. He now understood very well, he observed to himself in the lecture he was delivering in his head, what had driven his own father away from Monkscombe. The place bred an odious self-righteousness. Harriet loved the house, but he was beginning to see it as a monster. It fed off the Stantons. It turned them into creatures who had no other thought but that of serving it. Harriet had been brought up to devote her days and nights to Monkscombe, and she knew nothing else. The truly sad part of it was that, until now, she had not even realised that she knew nothing else. Now she might realise it, but the realisation had come too late.

The stableyard was dark, cold and deserted, but Ben was glad of the icy wind that blew across his perspiring forehead and cooled his anger. He crossed the cobbled yard, unhooked a lantern which swung by the stable and pushed open the door. The familiar, reassuring, warm, acrid smell of horses greeted him. He hung the lantern safely out of the way of any hay, and made his way down the line of stalls. Heads raised as he passed, and ears pricked curiously to know what he was doing there so late. He patted the nose of Harriet's chestnut cob, and observed softly to it, "Well, old fellow, your mistress and I are sadly at odds."

A creak and the sound of a footstep from the door caused him to look round. Joe Henderson's burly form filled the entrance. He peered suspiciously down the stable, asking, "Who the devil be that?"

"Only I, Joe," said Ben, and smiled wryly, thinking how strange Joe would think it to find a bridegroom skulking in the stables on his wedding night.

"Why, Mr. Stanton," said honest Joe, "I didn't think to find you here!" He came ponderously down the line of stalls. "Horses be all right. You've no cause to go worriting about they. Christmas or not Christmas, I don't leave my animals."

"You're not married, Joe?" Ben asked him.

"Not I!" said Joe sturdily. "I don't need no female chasing after me and telling I what to do all the danged day long. Horses, now, is sensible. Women ain't, that's my opinion." He seemed to reflect that this was not a suitable observation to a newly-married man, and added, "Ladies, I dare say, is different."

"Women, ladies or not, get a man into a pretty fair muddle, Joe," said Ben with a sigh, stroking the chestnut, which pushed its nose sympathetically into his chest. "A man thinks he's doing the right thing, and it seems he does the wrong one, whatever he does."

"It's a fact," agreed Joe. "You can leave I to bar the door, sir."

Ben took the hint. Joe might be a bachelor, but he had firm ideas on where a bridegroom belonged.

Ben bid the groom goodnight, and returned to the house. He made his way to his own room and his own solitary and celibate bed. It was a course of action which would have disgusted Joe, and—thought Ben, lying back on the pillows and putting his hands under his head—it seemed, just at this moment, a pretty bad idea all round, whichever way you looked at it.

IT WAS AS WELL that Christmas festivities followed. Everyone was concerned with eating and drinking and generally visiting around and dancing and making merry, so that, one way and another, no one gave much thought to the newly-weds.

Ben seemed to take it all in his stride, and no one seeing him would have thought anything amiss. Harriet tried her best, and must have been successful, she thought sadly, because no one asked her what was wrong.

She had to survive yet another humiliation on the occasion of Lady Williams's Christmas ball. They were obliged to attend, and to remain as house-guests for a whole three days. Not surprisingly Lady Williams, when making up the guest-lists, keeping in mind that here she had a young couple scarcely two weeks wed, put them in the same bedroom. Harriet's immediate thought was that here was a chance to put matters right. On their wedding night, he had declared his intention and obstinately stuck to it. But he had had a little time to mull it over, Harriet had tried to show herself suitably contrite, he could change his mind without loss of dignity, and surely, a whole night alone together...

She had underestimated his resolve. "Don't concern yourself," he said brusquely. "I'll sleep in the chair."

Harriet said meekly, "You really don't have to."

"I choose to," was the uncompromising retort.

She watched him pile pillows and blanket into the chair, as she climbed into the large, empty bed by herself. Ben blew out the candle, and she could hear him shifting awkwardly as he settled into his comfortless sleeping place. The first night she lay awake for some time, knowing he was awake also, and wondering if he would change his mind. The second night she ventured to ask into the darkness, "Are you all right?"

This brought the sharp retort, "Fine, thank you."

Harriet turned over and burrowed into the pillows, and thought, exasperated, that there really was nothing to be done with anyone as obstinate as that.

Ben, for his part, spent two nights virtually without any sleep, listening to Harriet's even breathing; thinking bitterly to himself that she must be without any sensitivity to sleep like a log while he was suffering cold discomfort; envying her the feather bed; wondering if, after all, he might not just creep in beside her and sternly rejecting the idea; drifting off into uneasy slumber and, in the morning, awaking feeling as if a herd of wild mustang had careered over every joint and muscle in his body.

But eventually Christmas was over, and Mr. Ferrar reluctantly informed them that he must return to Bristol. He could not, he said, remember when he had enjoyed Christmas more. The cook at Monkscombe had surpassed herself. To listen to Miss Caroline sing and play was a delight. He was, above all, happy to know that Harriet was settled.

Harriet, to whom he said all this, looked singularly gloomy, and replied that she was very glad he had enjoyed himself. As her words and her manner contradicted one another so obviously that even Mr. Ferrar could not ignore it, he gave her a shrewd look, sighed, and observed,

"My dear girl, I've known you all your life. What is troubling you now? I must say I had hoped to see you looking rather happier than you do. In the circumstances..."

Mr. Ferrar fell into a somewhat embarrassed silence. He was forgetting that the girl might be experiencing some difficulty in adjusting to the idea of being married. Without wishing to pry in an indelicate manner, there was that tiresome business which generally resulted in the arrival of bouncing babies. It had not done so in the case of Mr. Ferrar and his late, lamented wife—but then Jonas had never really felt at ease about the matter—an over-rated pastime, in his opinion. Also the late Mrs. Ferrar, an excellent housewife and good woman, had not been quite what...

Ben Stanton probably thought differently. Most young fellows did. And Harriet certainly would inspire a great deal more ardour than the last Mrs. Ferrar. But the young fellow might well have given way to an excess of enthusiasm, understandable enough, and not realise how new it all was to the girl. She might be a little distressed. After all, the—ah—novelty, not to say, um, shock... Jonas said cautiously, "I know you have a husband to confide in now, but perhaps I might still provide a shoulder to cry on?"

He was not prepared for her to take this invitation quite literally. To his great dismay, she burst into tears, flung her arms around him, and cried out, "Oh, Jonas, I was never so unhappy in all my life!"

"Oh dear, oh dear," muttered Mr. Ferrar, patting her shoulder and thinking wistfully of his snuffbox. "Has it been as bad as that?" Privately, he thought, what the deuce has the fellow been doing to her? Aloud, he soothed, "Oh dear, well, I dare say... These things take some getting used to, Harriet. An awkward and embarrassing experience at first—as I well recall... But you know, in time..."

"Oh, no!" she wailed. "That isn't it at all!" And then the whole sorry tale spilled out, interspersed with sobs and hiccups.

Mr. Ferrar listened in mounting alarm and increasing dismay. His fingers searched automatically for that old friend in need, his snuffbox, and fiddled with it absently. "My dear child..." he said. "What can I say? I never imagined—no, not at all. A fine, healthy young fellow like that—what's the matter with him?" demanded the lawyer in sudden suspicion.

"Nothing!" sobbed Harriet. "It's all my fault."

"Nonsense!" he declared robustly. "Of course it isn't!" He sighed. "Indeed, Harriet, if it is anyone's fault, it is mine. I confess I thought I could arrange things to everyone's satisfaction and benefit. He seemed so suitable... You are a very attractive girl... I did not see how it could fail to be anything but an excellent match." He tucked the snuffbox away in his waistcoat pocket. "Harriet, I must tell you that there is no fool like an old fool, and I am just such an old fool. I had forgot, you see, that a young man does not think in the way an old one does. The fellow wished to secure the future of a pair of unprotected women, and one must respect him for that. I admit it was I who suggested to him the means by which he might do it. I was not wrong to ask him to do his duty, but I was quite wrong to ask him to give his heart. That is another matter altogether. He is an honourable young fellow, and I don't doubt he does not wish to play fast and loose with your affections..."

Although, thought Mr. Ferrar wrathfully, observing Harriet's dejected figure, he seems to be doing so pretty thoroughly, whether he intends it or not!

"Well, there it is," he concluded. "But now what is to be done about it, that's the thing."

"I don't think there is anything to be done, Jonas," said Harriet dolefully.

"Now look here," said Mr. Ferrar, straightening his wig, and adopting a militant posture, "it's not begun well, but might still end well. Give the fellow a little encouragement, Harriet. If he has any blood in his veins at all, he won't need much."

"You see," said Harriet, wiping her eyes and making an attempt to pull herself together—an effort that contained so much desperate courage that Mr. Ferrar pulled out his own handkerchief and blew his nose noisily. "I have hurt his pride. I was so unwelcoming, and said such awful things. I don't know why I did it.

He will not forgive me, you know. He is very obstinate."

"*Nil desperandum*, Harriet!" ordered Mr. Ferrar. "You will not give up. I never knew you to give up. Now then, do you want me to talk to the fellow?"

"Oh, no!" she cried, growing very agitated. "Not for the world."

"Very well," he said. "I can't say I go back to Bristol very happy, but there..."

"It is not your fault, Jonas, you did what you did for the best," she told him. She got up from her chair and walked over to the window. "I always believed, you know, that Monkscombe meant more to me than anything else in the world, except, perhaps, Caroline's happiness. Now Monkscombe doesn't seem very important any more. It is very odd."

And another thing I had forgot, thought Mr. Ferrar, watching her face. I had forgot what a very painful thing it is to be in love.

CHAPTER SEVEN

JONAS HAD GONE. The Christmas holly that had
caused its own little upset had been taken down and
blazed merrily on the gardener's bonfire. Monkscombe had resumed its usual appearance and fallen
back into its accustomed routine, and the situation
between Harriet and Ben slowly began to take on the
semblance of normality. She became used to hearing
herself called "Mrs. Stanton", even though the title
could not lose its hollow ring. But their behaviour towards each other was outwardly polite and civilised.
Ben consulted her fairly frequently about estate business, and she ought, she supposed, to consider her
situation a comfortable one.

In reality, her situation was an increasingly intoler-
able one. The longer it went on, the more permanent
it became, and the more difficult it would be to change
it. But perhaps Ben also found it more of a trial than
he showed. Without warning, he announced that he
would be going to Bristol and might stay there for
some little time. He would leave the following day.

Early though the hour was, Harriet went out on to
the portico steps the next morning and waited for him
to ride round the corner of the house on his way from
the stableyard to the main drive. When he appeared,
she pulled the shawl tightly about her and stepped
forward.

Ben reined up in front of her and leaned forward with his arms crossed across the pommel of the saddle, looking at her questioningly. The horse tossed its head and stamped an impatient hind hoof on the frosty gravel, and blew smoky breath into the cold air. It was one of those crisp, cold, clear winter mornings. The bare twigs of nearby bushes were rimmed with a tinsel-like silver trimming of frost, and spiders' webs were picked out like lace.

Harriet said awkwardly, "I only came to wish you a safe journey."

She looked almost insignificant in the shadow of the portico, small and slightly built and incredibly vulnerable. Ben shifted his weight in the saddle and glanced up at the house behind her. Its shape brooded over them both like a crouching animal, and he knew then that deep inside his heart he hated it.

Aloud, he said, "You'll take cold, go inside." His tone sounded almost brutal to his own ears, ringing icily on the frosty air. She stepped back a pace or two, and it seemed to him almost as if he had struck her. For the briefest, most fleeting, of moments he felt like reaching out and dragging her up on to the horse behind him, and taking her off to Bristol with him, clinging to him as she had done before.

But the moment passed. She had no wish to be anywhere but here, Monkscombe. He said, "I'll write and let you know where I lodge." Then he jerked hard on the reins, swinging round the startled horse, and set off for the gates at a great rate, silvered gravel grit flying up beneath the animal's hoofs.

FOR A FEW DAYS, Harriet tried to carry on as though nothing were amiss, but her heart was not in it. It seemed that matters could only go from bad to worse. One person only was constantly on her mind. Ben is in Bristol, and I don't know what he is doing, or even what business took him there, she thought. Meantime, here I sit at Monkscombe and listen to complaints from tenants that their roofs leak, or do the rector's sick round for him. All the world can see that my husband has deserted me within a few weeks of marriage. They probably all wonder what I have done to drive him away.

All the time, the one thought ran through her brain: When the year is up, and Ben goes back to America for good, I shall be left here, like this, for the rest of my life. Yet a life at Monkscombe was what I always wanted . . .

Towards the end of the week, as she was returning from the kitchen garden towards the house, she heard the clatter of approaching hoofs. Her heart leapt up for a moment, hoping it would be Ben, returned already, but it was James Murray. He swung down from the saddle and bid her goodday.

"I suppose you have come to see my sister," she said with a resigned smile.

He scraped his boots on the path, and mumbled, "I asked permission of Mr. Stanton, and he was kind enough to grant it . . ." He looked up and met her eyes with youthful frankness. "But I dare say you don't care for my coming very much, Mrs. Stanton. You would wish better for Caroline, and I don't blame you."

Harriet sighed. "We all like you very much, James, but life is so often a matter of shillings and pence. I know you want to marry Caro, but however would the pair of you live? And if you had children, you know, the difficulties would be so much more. Caro has lived all her life here in comfort. She's never had to count the cost of anything she's ever wanted. Our late father was the most indulgent of parents, and my—my husband has willingly paid Caroline's bills of late. I don't doubt Caro's affection for you, but she just wouldn't know how to live in lodgings or in any way modestly. I know you cling to this idea of seeking a regular commission, but surely you must see that garrison life just is not for my sister?''

''Yes, I know it,'' he burst out. ''But I can't offer her anything else!''

There was so much youthful despair in his voice that it wrenched at Harriet's heart. She realised that here was someone as least as unhappy as she was. Impulsively, she seized his hand and exclaimed, ''Dear James! Please don't despair. Surely we must be able to find some way...''

''It is no use my staying in the county,'' he said obstinately. ''My family is not a local one, as you know, and I have no one here to speak for me or ensure my preferment. I shall kick my heels as a captain of local militia, chasing after smugglers and invisible spies, until I'm too old and stiff to clamber into the saddle, and that's the truth of it. I have written to my father in Scotland, and explained my situation. But while he understands my wish to be married, he is quite unable to do anything for me. My eldest brother has lately married, and my second eldest brother ran himself into debt and cost my father a great deal to clear his losses. I am left on my own and must muddle through in any way I can, and that's that.''

Harriet cast about feverishly in her mind for some solution to this apparently insoluble problem. ''How would it be if Caroline remained here for a year or two after you married, just while you were establishing your army career? Until you got promotion and were better able to provide for her?''

He stared at her aghast. ''That's no good! Begging your pardon, Mrs. Stanton, because I know you mean it kindly. But what's the use of being married if you're not together?''

''None at all,'' said Harriet dully. ''You had better go and find Caroline.''

She watched him set off to the house and thought, How foolish I was even to try to secure my future and Caro's by marrying Ben. I can't keep Caro at Monkscombe. Ben was quite right to warn me that we cannot run other people's lives for them. She will marry James in the end, and he will take her off to some dreadful garrison town, and she will lose all her looks and her vivacity and not even have her music to console her. As for me, what is the use of Monkscombe without Ben? It is as James says: it is no use being married if we are not together.

She followed James into the house with a heavy heart.

AS SO OFTEN when the hour seems blackest, an ally proved unexpectedly at hand. He appeared in the unlikely shape of Sir Mortimer Fish. A groom rode over, sent by the magistrate, to tell the ladies at Monkscombe that Sir Mortimer was obliged to travel to Bristol on business. If there was anything he could do for either of them while he was there, they should let him know. He would be happy to be the bearer of letters from Mrs. Stanton to her husband.

Harriet seized the opportunity as heaven-sent, and made a decision without a second thought. "Take a letter? Indeed not. He shall take *me!*"

She sat down and scribbled a note, begging Sir Mortimer to call at the house, as she would deem it a great favour if he would kindly give her a place in his carriage to Bristol. She then ran upstairs and began to thrust necessary personal items feverishly into a bag, watched by Caroline.

"Ben will be surprised to see you, and I'm sure delighted," said Caroline innocently. "He must miss you as much as you miss him. I'm sure I should hate to be separated from my husband when I'd only just been married."

Harriet paused in thrusting linen into her portmanteau, and frowned. Ben would be surprised, all right, but not particularly delighted. She grew thoughtful. It might be as well if Ben did not know straight away that she was in Bristol. She could go and stay with an old school friend who was married and living in the city. Susan would be very pleased to see her, and Harriet could make discreet enquiries about what Ben was doing before appearing before him. To some people, that might sound like spying on him. If so, Ben could hardly complain. Had he not, when he first arrived at Monkscombe, spied on them from the coppice? Nor should I have been obliged to do it, thought Harriet militantly, if Ben had behaved well and taken me with him—or explained properly what he was going there to do.

Bristol lay half a day's travel distant, on a lonely, hazardous road made more treacherous by winter rains. Mud clogged up the wheels and coated the struggling horses. It was flung up and splattered the windows so that it was difficult to see out. Harriet knew they were following the coast along the eastern side of the Bristol Channel. It was hugging this coast-line and sailing in the opposite direction that a boat had crept to rendezvous at the mouth of the Channel with the French ship and to take off the spy, Lesage. It was a bold and ingenious scheme. Few French ships troubled to sail in these waters. British naval patrols were so much the scarcer. There were excisemen, but they were few and scattered. The natives were tradi-tionally at odds with the law. Informers were almost unknown, and had anyone broken the unwritten code, he would have disappeared without trace. Somewhere out there in the wild countryside that Harriet could just discern through the mud-caked windows, Lesage lay hidden.

To make this journey in a cold carriage in the com-pany of a deaf octogenarian, fortifying himself at in-tervals from a hip-flask, across a winter landscape of badly rutted roads, was not the most congenial or comfortable, but Harriet bore it well. As the carriage drew away further and further from Monkscombe, her spirits began to rise and a sense of adventure took hold of her. At Monkscombe, things had not gone well be-tween Ben and herself. But away from the house, everything might be different. The looming and al-most oppressive presence of the house itself, and all it represented, would be absent. She and Ben would be just two people able to sit and talk over their differ-ences and the problems in their situation. Susan, with whom she meant to stay, had been married some five or six years, and it might also help to talk things over with her, and gain advice on how to manage a husband. All in all, Harriet entered Bristol feeling highly optimistic.

SUSAN WAS especially pleased to see her, because her husband, a naval officer, was away at sea at the moment.

"It is not that I have time to be bored," she observed, seizing the baby by his petticoats before he tumbled into the fire. "The children have me running around the house all day. You've no idea how difficult it is, Harriet, to keep a reliable nursemaid. The girls are always going off and getting married themselves. Young Tom was four last week, and I never know what he is going to do next. Baby is just walking, as you see, and I really think I need eyes in the back of my head. But what I do miss so, when Tom is away, is someone to talk to of an evening. I do hope you will stay a little while, Harriet."

Susan's Tom might be absent in the flesh but he was very much present in the spirit. On the wall hung his likeness, painted just before he left and declared by his doting wife to be quite like him, "only making him look a little stern, which really he is not." His slippers stood in the hearth, awaiting their owner's return. His young son climbed upon Harriet's knee and regaled her with endless hair-raising accounts of the taking of French prizes in which his papa had played a gallant role. In fact, to listen to Young Tom, one might wonder how the British Navy could ever manage without his papa.

When bedtime finally came, Harriet accompanied Susan upstairs to hear Master Tom recite his prayers, requesting God to keep his papa safe from storm, sea-monsters, the French guns, mutiny, pirates, getting lost because the charts were wrong, and "also, please God, that he don't get eaten by a shark."

After this the two friends were able to come downstairs, the maid brought in the tea-tray, Susan pinned on her lace cap straight, and they settled down for a good gossip.

What Harriet had to tell at first struck Susan dumb. She then asked increduously, "What—not at all, ever—I mean, not even on your wedding night?"

"Never, not once," said Harriet with a sigh. "He thinks that all I wanted was the house, which isn't surprising, because I told him so. Now he says I have what I want, and that's enough. But it isn't enough, Susan. For what I now know I really want is a home like yours, with children, and Ben in it. But how is it ever to be, if our marriage is to remain on paper only?"

"Well, I must say," observed Susan, "that it's an arrangement which wouldn't suit Tom at all. To be perfectly frank, Harriet, I can't think it really suits Mr. Stanton. But he has got himself into a corner, you see, with taking the stand that he has, and he can't get out of it. Men are so obstinate. I know Tom is. It is no use expecting them to admit they are wrong, you know, or to confess to having made a mistake." She picked up a broken toy and thoughtfully placed the halves together to see if it could be glued. "Sometimes they can be mended," she observed, which followed on a little oddly from her main theme.

"It is a question," said Harriet gloomily, "of whether my marriage can be mended."

"Oh, Harriet dear," exclaimed Susan, taking hold of her hand, "why ever not? It's a lovers' quarrel. He is upset because you seemed to care so much more for the house than for him. A husband likes to be first in his wife's affections. You must let him see that you care more for him."

"But he doesn't care for me," argued Harriet. "At least, not in that way. He takes care to be polite, and I dare say in marrying me, he meant to be kind. But I don't think he sees me as a woman at all. I am just Harriet, and a nuisance."

Susan rescued the toast, propped under the fender and about to singe, and piled it on Harriet's plate. "A man doesn't go marrying a girl out of charity, Harriet. I don't care what you say. I dare say he would love you if you would let him. And if he doesn't have that idea in his head yet, well then, you must put it there."

THE FOLLOWING MORNING, Harriet emerged from the house, warmly clad against the chill wind and with a veil draped over her bonnet to hide her face. She made her way early to the hostelry where Ben lodged. She could not enter boldy and enquire for him, so she hung about in the vicinity, gazing in shop windows and buying reels of thread she didn't need, until she was rewarded with the sight of Ben leaving, and setting off briskly down the street.

Harriet made a precipitate exit from the shop where she was bargaining half-heartedly over a length of muslin that the shopkeeper was prepared to reduce in price, as it was winter, and set off in hot pursuit. It was not easy. He walked very fast and took much longer strides than she could. But his height helped, and somehow or other she managed to keep him in sight. Eventually they arrived on the wharves where the city's shipping was busy about its business. Here it was more difficult to keep sight of Ben, as the area was so crowded, and the pavements strewn with all kinds of obstacles in the way of chests of tea and bales and boxes of all sorts. There were also some very strange-looking people about: seamen and porters, shipping clerks and warehousemen, and women of a very brash appearance, in brightly coloured petticoats and with painted faces, who shouted boldly at passers-by.

Fortunately, most people were too busy to pay much attention to her. She had already decided on a story to tell if she were stopped and questioned. She would be enquiring for a long-lost younger brother who had run away to sea. She had embroidered this tale in her head to such an extent already that she almost believed in the missing youth. Then she saw that Ben, ahead of her, had stopped. She slipped into the doorway of a chandlers' store and peered out between coils of rope, boxes of tallow candles and a variety of objects whose purpose she could not even guess at.

Ben was staring up at a ship moored alongside the wharf. She was being loaded, and a procession of brawny men passed up and down her gangplank, laden with bundles. As one of these came down, free of his burden, Ben stopped him and appeared to ask some question. The man rubbed his chin and glanced back at the ship behind him. A deep conversation then ensued, which concluded with Ben giving the seaman some coin by way of recompense. He then resumed his walk. Harriet left the security of the doorway, and followed after.

This sort of process was repeated two or three times. Ben stopped seamen and talked to them, asking quesitons, paying for the information he received. Once he took out a spyglass from his coat pocket and studied a ship more closely, before closing up the instrument with a snap and turning to enter a tavern.

Harriet sat down on a coil of rope, and turned it all over in her mind. What on earth was he about? Why was he so interested in the shipping? What kind of information did he seek from the men he had questioned? Despite herself, a niggle of her old suspicions of him crept back into her mind. It was a very odd business. The Frenchman, Lesage, had never been found. Ben had arrived at the very moment Lesage had disappeared. The descriptions of the two men tallied, in as far as any description of the Frenchman was to hand. Ben had come to them from Europe, ostensibly from Vienna. But Vienna was currently in the hands of the French. Harriet's heart sank. Was it indeed possible that her husband, the heir to Monkscombe and a Stanton, was a French spy?

Whatever should she do? She could not tell any of this to Susan. Susan's Tom was a naval man, and Susan's first instinct would be to run to the authorities with a report of possible espionage. She could perhaps tell Jonas? But Jonas had treated all her suspicions of Ben as fanciful. As she sat there, Harriet suddenly heard the sound of shrill female laughter, and looking up, saw approaching a pair of girls of the kind she had noticed about here already. They were well if rather vulgarly dressed, and marched down the quayside arm in arm, exchanging ribald banter with the seamen. Before the tavern they stopped, consulted together and then disappeared inside.

Harriet longed to follow them, but if she did so, Ben would surely see her. Besides, it was not the sort of place into which respectable women went. She got up and went to peer through the dusty windowpanes. It was dark and gloomy inside, and the air thick with the smoke from clay-pipes. Her view was obscured by the backs on the two jades, who stood in the middle of the taproom surveying the customers. Abruptly they parted company. One went to the left, and out of Harriet's line of sight. The other made a bee-line for a table in the corner, and a man who sat there alone.

It was Ben. Harriet clenched her fists in impotent fury. The wretched girl was leaning over him and hailing him in a familiar manner. The drab even reached out and patted his cheek, obviously making some invitation, the nature of which was plain enough. "Hussy!" seethed Harriet silently. "Get away from my husband!" She fairly danced on the pavement with impatience and longed to rush in and pull the girl away. Then she thought, Ben can take care of himself, surely, and send the girl packing. Harriet pressed her nose to the glass and waited for him to do so.

He did not do so. He made a gesture with his hand, inviting the girl to sit down. The girl plumped herself down opposite him, leaned her arms on the table, and propped an ample bosom on them.

"Flaunting herself under his nose like that!" fumed Harriet. "Jezebel!"

The two at the table were now deep in conversation. Without warning, they stood up. Harriet scuttled away from the window and dived behind a stack of tea-chests marked "Best Bohea". The tavern door opened and Ben came out, the girl hanging on his arm. Far from sending her packing, he was laughing at her teasing prattle, and to Harriet's horror and dismay the pair of them disappeared down an alley. Harriet crept out, dusting Best Bohea from her sleeves, and trotted determinedly after. Peering round the corner, she was just in time to see them enter an establishment that maintained a discreet frontage and was guarded at the door by a man with cauliflower ears. Into this man's hand Ben pressed a coin. The guardian of the door bit the coin, and pocketed it. The door slammed, and the girl and Ben were lost to view.

"Miserable wretch!" muttered Harriet, hopping about from foot to foot in rage. "Taking up with a painted hussy! I am scorned, and that—that creature is preferred! I hope they rob him of his pocket-book!" She stormed off in a red mist of fury, leaving Ben to his illicit pleasures. She might have reflected that, while what we do not know does us no harm— what we obstinately insist on finding out often causes us a great deal of heartache.

BEN, RETURNING LATER to his lodgings, would not have given anyone to guess that he had been enjoying himself. He strode along with his hands in his pockets, his broad shoulders hunched against the chill wind, and a scowl on his face. The business he had come to Bristol to conduct was progressing well enough, but in other ways his visit was depressing. A large, busy, strange city is a lonely place, especially in wintertime. During the day he kept occupied enough, but night drew in early, and then there was little to do but go to bed and lie there wondering what Harriet was doing.

It was odd how often his thoughts returned to Monkscombe. He missed the place more than he would have thought possible. He had even begun to wish that he had, after all, asked Harriet to come along to Bristol with him, just to have someone to talk to. He was obliged to admit that he missed both her company and Caroline's—but Harriet's especially. At this point he would sit up and thump the pillow robustly with his fist in an attempt to get comfortable. He never seemed to be able to achieve any measure of comfort. It was the worst bed he had ever slept in. He twisted one way and another, and got irritable and tired—and tired, especially, of having nothing there but his own company. Occasionally he stretched out his bare foot experimentally into the empty space beside him, but it was cold, unwelcoming and untenanted. He threw himself over from his left side to his right, though it was in no way more comfortable, and made a determined effort to go to sleep.

But he remained wide awake, and blamed it on the dinner he had eaten, unquestionably one of the worst ever cooked. He had not thought so at the time, but he did now. He tossed over from right side to left, getting hopelessly entangled in the bedclothes, kicked the whole lot on the floor, got out of bed and piled them on again, crawled back in, muttering, and began to think about Harriet again. He hoped she was coping all right, and that the wretched Pardy was not hanging about the place. He ought not, perhaps, to have left her. The memory of her small, dejected figure, so bravely putting a brave face on things, lurking in the shadow of the portico to bid him goodbye, haunted him. He was not worried about Caroline, because that was not where Aaron's interest lay, and anyway, wherever Caro went she was accompanied by the loyal James. But Harriet, for all Ben knew, was driving all round the estate in that gig, and being waylaid in every lonely lane by a disreputable runner of contraband with but one thought on his mind. Ben sat up and pummelled the pillow until the feathers flew.

He threw himself down on his back and glowered up into the darkness. From below came the distant, muffled sound of roistering. He could not think what had possessed him to take a room at this inn. It was the noisiest he had ever been in. He began to think about Harriet again, and some of the thoughts quite surprised him. He rolled over on his side and slid his hand across the mattress, and wished it would encounter another body, perhaps one in particular. He would then fall into a restless slumber, and wake to find he had both arms wrapped round the pillow.

All this frustration—none of which he could quite satisfactorily explain—had an inevitable result. He had, this afternoon, succumbed to the blandishments of common street doxy, and now, as he strode through the streets, reflected on the episode with regret. At the time the girl had appeared pretty and her conversation pert and amusing. A passing need had been satisfied adequately enough, and he ought in theory to feel more relaxed. Instead, he felt worse, and disgusted as well. Looking back, the girl was cheap, tawdry and none too well washed. The room to which she had taken him had been stale and stuffy, the sheets creased and stained, the whole atmosphere seamy and distasteful to him. She knew her business, that girl, no one could complain about that. But her affection was false, her embraces were those of a professional whore, meaningless, a poor substitute for the real thing, and left him wanting to get out of there as quickly as possible and take a bath.

As he shouldered his way purposefully through the crowds, he was aware that his name was being called.

He stopped and glanced round and saw that a carriage drawn up at the side of the street held an ancient gentleman who leaned out at a perilous angle and gesticulated wildly at him with an ear-trumpet.

"Stanton!" squawked Sir Mortimer. "Over here, sir!" He burst into a fit of coughing and fell back into the interior of the coach.

Ben ran across the road, dodging other vehicles, and put his head through the door. Sir Mortimer was collapsed on a seat, but did not appear to have suffered a heart attack. He signalled, wheezing, that Ben should climb in and take the seat opposite to him. Ben did so.

"Saw you..." gasped Sir Mortimer, regaining his breath. "Standing about in the street no good, damn cold wind. Here, have a drop of this." He fumbled at his side and produced a bottle, which he passed across. "Friend of mine sends it to me from Jamaica—got a sugar plantation. They make the stuff."

Ben unstoppered the bottle and sniffed cautiously. The fumes made his eyes water. "Jumping Jehoshaphat!" he muttered, startled, "this is White Lightning!"

"Keeps the cold away," said Sir Mortimer, eyeing him with satisfaction. "Go on, get it down you."

Ben took a cautious gulp, choked, and hastily returned the bottle. Sir Mortimer re-stoppered it and placed it carefully in his pocket. "Can't stand city life myself. Prefer the country. Too much hustle and bustle, at my time of life, can't be doing with it."

Ben ventured to ask him just how old he was.

"Eighty-six," said Sir Mortimer with glee. "Born four years after the Old Pretender made a try for the throne, and I was twenty-six, sir, when the Young

Pretender came over. I was present, sir, at the engagement of Culloden. Ah,'' said Sir Mortimer reminiscently, "men knew how to drink in those days. Never sober in the saddle, that was the motto of any officer or gentleman. Neither would you have wanted to be quite sober, faced with a horde of mad Scotsmen all half-naked, shrieking and laying about them with claymores. I took, however, a fancy for the Scottish drink of whisky. Very fine, sir, though not equal of a good French brandy.'' Sir Mortimer cleared his throat as though he had recollected that fine French brandies were not supposed to be easily available at the present time. "I have, Stanton," he declared, "reached my present great age, keeping myself in excellent health, by one simple rule. Never go to bed sober, that's it. I recommend it to you.''

"I'll bear it in mind," Ben told him.

"What's brought you here?'' enquired Sir Mortimer genially.

"Shipping, sir. *Shipping!* I am making enquiry about cargo ships. For my business—*my business*! Oh, good Lord... I have been to enquire at the docks, one can't always trust the shipping agents. Best to take a look at the ships at berth. *Berth*, sir!''

"Already?'' exclaimed Sir Mortimer. "Bit early for births, ain't it? Mind you, it won't be the first infant to get itself into the world ahead of time. Somewhat of a rush for the altar, was it?''

"Not that kind of birth!'' howled Ben. "Ships' berths!''

"What?'' His companion leaned forward, brandishing the ear-trumpet. "Where is your good lady? Shopping, I'll be bound. Women have a great deal of fondness for spending a man's money. But she ought

not to be out and about in this cold wind in her con-
dition. Not if you are expecting the birth so soon. I
believe I was married once," said Sir Mortimer,
frowning and looking vague. "But nothing came of it.
As I recall, she was a dreadful, plain female with a
long nose and a longer tongue." He took out the bottle of White Lightning and poured a generous measure into a silver beaker. "Your health, sir."

"Mrs. Stanton is at Monkscombe!" Ben bellowed.

Sir Mortimer coughed and wiped his mouth. "No,
she ain't. Brought her to Bristol myself. Tell you what,
Stanton, you've mislaid her, that's what. It's easily
done. Don't blame yourself. Busy city like Bristol.
Other things on your mind. You turn around and she's
gone, and you've no idea where you left her. I mislaid
my wife somewhere or other. Or, at least, one day she
was there and the next she wasn't. Never did find her.
But don't worry, boy, I dare say Harriet will turn up.
Sensible sort of gel, and will find her way home. Give
a good mare her head, turn her loose, and she'll make
straight for her own stable every time."

"Sir Mortimer!" Ben bawled into the ear-trumpet,
not sure just how drunk the old sinner was, or whether
White Lightning had done for his wits. "Are you quite
sure you brought my wife to Bristol? Perhaps it was on
some other occasion?"

"No, no," said Sir Mortimer huffily. "I recollect,
most particular, setting her down in the street."

"Which street?" roared Ben.

"Bless me, young fellow, not the slightest notion.
Ask my coachman."

"I will!" promised Ben with some emotion, and
leapt out of the carriage.

YOUNG TOM WAS OBJECTING to his bath. From downstairs his roaring could plainly be heard, interspersed with the pleas and rebukes of his nurse and his mama. Harriet sat before the fire, with Baby on her knees, attempting to feed him mashed rusk. Baby was being weaned. It was not an easy matter. He disliked mashed rusk, and as fast as she filled his mouth, he would allow it to dribble out. Harriet sighed, patiently scooped up the rejected food and re-inserted it into Baby, who varied his approach by holding it all in his mouth until his red cheeks were distended like bellows and then spat it all out in one mouthful.

Above the noise of Tom's yells, and concentrating though she was on outwitting Baby, Harriet became aware of a further uproar in the house. It came from the hall, where, it seemed, some visitor was demanding admittance. She was wondering whether to put down Baby and go and see what was amiss, when a familiar voice thundered, "Confound it, I have come for my wife!"

The door flew open and Ben burst in, much dishevelled, with his hat in hand. He came to a halt, pointed the hat accusingly at her, and demanded, "What in tarnation are you doing here?"

"Why, helping Susan," said Harriet with as much sangfroid as she could manage. "How did you know I was here?"

"I met Sir Mortimer. I thought at first he was half-seas-over, but he insisted he had set you down in Bristol—what are you doing here?"

"I have come to visit an old friend," Harriet said. "I take it you have no objection?"

Ben paused and glared at her somewhat baffled. No, he had no objection. She could, he supposed, visit her friends. He began to suspect that his anger was making him look and sound foolish. He drew himself up, and fixed Harriet with a stern eye. The light was fading and the rosy firelight flickered on her face. She looked extremely pretty, even though—or perhaps even because—she was wearing an apron, and clasping a robust infant with mashed rusk all over its face. Ben struggled to maintain his dignified mien.

"Put that baby down!" he ordered.

Harriet attempted to, but Baby clung to her with clenched fists and rightly regarding Ben as an interloper, pulled faces at him. "I can't," she said. "He will cry. It is his supper-time."

"Hasn't he a nursemaid or something?" Exasperated, Ben took the chair opposite and stuck out his booted feet before the fire, letting his hat fall on to the carpet.

"She is upstairs with Susan, because Young Tom won't get into the bath." Harriet scooped up a spoonful of mashed rusk. "Come along, Baby, just one, for Aunt Harriet . . ." she wheedled.

"If you had said you wanted to come and visit your friend," Ben said crossly, "you could have travelled to Bristol with me."

"You didn't ask."

Ben grunted. Baby solved the rusk problem by abruptly falling asleep in Harriet's arms. She pushed the bowl aside and sat back, rocking him gently. Ben stirred in his chair and watched her moodily for some minutes. Eventually, he said rather resentfully, "I could have done with your company."

"Could you, indeed?" said Harriet archly. "You do surprise me."

He glowered at her. "What is that supposed to mean?"

"Oh, I thought you would have been much too busy. What is your business in Bristol?"

"Nothing of interest to you," Ben said briefly.

"Perhaps it is indeed something you would rather not discuss," said Harriet, pushing back a lock of stray curls with one hand, and cuddling Baby with the other.

Ben leaned forward, his jaw jutting pugnaciously, and growled, "That's the second time you've dropped hints. What do you think I've been doing?"

"It's not my concern," returned Harriet, growing agitated. "But it is hardly very pleasant to see one's husband arm in arm with a loose woman in broad daylight where anyone can see him!"

His face went red, and then it went white. He said hoarsely, "Well, I'll be... You have been spying on me!"

"Then you have had some of your own medicine!" Harriet snapped accusingly.

"I will not be spied on and quizzed!" he shouted, jumping to his feet.

Baby opened his eyes and burst into howls. "Now see what you've done!" cried Harriet.

"You will go back to Monkscombe!" Ben panted. "You will... Can't you stop that child yelling? You will go back to Monkscombe tomorrow. I'll make arrangements and send a conveyance for you. Harriet, will you put that baby down?"

"No, I will not! I like him."

"If you wanted a child that much," said Ben cuttingly, "you should have told me so when I asked you if there was anything you wanted besides Monkscombe. I could have arranged for you to have both!''

"You flatter yourself!" snapped Harriet. "For a man who has never been anywhere near his wife's bed, you have the most extraordinary conceit!"

"A man would have to be as deaf as Sir Mortimer to get into your bed," snarled Ben, "because you'd be lecturing him the whole time he was there! You'd be as welcoming as a block of wood. Perhaps, when we get back to Monkscombe, Sir Mortimer will send over a bottle of his White Lightning, and if I get drunk enough, I'll consider it!"

"Get out of here!" stormed Harriet.

"W-aaa!" screeched Baby.

"You will go home tomorrow, madam!" shouted Ben, grabbing his hat and gesticulating furiously at her with it. "Tomorrow, do you hear?"

"Goodness me," said Susan brightly from the door, "it must be Mr. Stanton! What a pleasant surprise. Harriet has told me so much about you."

Ben whirled round, and Harriet was quite afraid for the moment that he was going to have an apoplectic fit. He managed to pull himself together, however, and apologise to Susan for invading her house.

"Not at all," declared Susan, descending on them and scooping up Baby. "Jane shall take Baby up to the nursery, and I'll ring for the tea-tray."

"I beg your pardon, ma'am," said Ben in a strangled voice, "but I must forgo the pleasure. Excuse me, ma'am... Harriet, tomorrow!" With this, he made an abrupt departure, marked by a slam of the front door.

"Dear me," said Susan, "why did you not say? He is very handsome!"

"He is very angry," said Harriet apprehensively.

"Oh yes, he's very angry," said her friend compla-
cently. "But don't tell me, Harriet," Susan wagged an
admonishing finger, "that he doesn't *care*."

CHAPTER EIGHT

KNOWING THAT Ben was a man of his word, Harriet packed her bag that evening. Sure enough, the hired carriage arrived at Susan's door the following morning. For a moment, she almost rebelled and sent it away, but Susan counselled caution.

"You must allow him to win this battle, Harriet. That will take care of his anger. You'll see, in a little while he will begin to think he was too harsh and want to make amends."

Harriet was not altogether convinced of this, but bowed to Susan's experience in managing a husband, and allowed herself to be borne back to Monks-combe.

She did not know it, but Ben lurked in a doorway at the corner of the street to watch her departure. He had half expected her to send the carriage away, and was mildly surprised to see her obey his orders without demur. To tell the truth, his conscience had begun to trouble him a little. She had no business to spy on him, but he could have explained himself better. He was sorry, too, to have wrenched her away from Susan's, where she had obviously been enjoying herself. When he returned to Monkscombe, he thought, he would suggest that she invite Susan and her children to stay for a while. This idea salved his conscience and he set out for Jonas Ferrar's offices.

He still did not feel entirely at ease. He began to think he had been hasty. It would have done no harm to allow Harriet to remain in Bristol, where he could have kept an eye on her, and known both that she was safe and what she was doing. He also felt strangely bereft, as though he had lost something, and arrived at the lawyer's offices in no very good mood.

Mr. Ferrar watched his visitor's tall frame as he paced restlessly up and down the congested little room. The lawyer's gaze grew shrewd, he patted his waistcoat for the snuffbox, and courteously offered it.

"Thank'ee, no," Ben said shortly.

Mr. Ferrar helped himself to a liberal pinch, tucked away the snuffbox, patted his wig to make sure it was straight, and spoke. "I have a confession to make to you, Stanton."

Ben stopped pacing, whirled round on his heel and stared at him.

"I fear I had forgot, when I advised you as I did, what a very difficult relationship marriage was. Alas, I am no expert," said Mr. Ferrar regretfully. "I have been thirty years a widower. Before that, I was not unhappily married; my late wife had some excellent qualities, but the union lacked a certain passion. Her father had made a considerable fortune in tea, and she brought me a fine sum by way of portion, not to mention a house, four chests of linen and an entire tea-service in Chinese porcelain. I don't wish to suggest that I married her for her worldly goods, but I admit that they led me to overlook how very plain she was." He sighed. "Harriet, of course, is a very attractive girl."

"I'm aware of it," Ben said briefly.

"I really wish that you would sit down," murmured the lawyer. "It is very difficult to talk to someone who is constantly on the move."

Ben apologised and threw himself down in a chair opposite, stretching out his long legs and folding his arms in an uncompromising attitude.

"I wonder..." said Mr. Ferrar, as if he had just thought of it. "I wonder if anyone has ever told you the circumstances of the quarrel that led to your late father quitting this country for America."

Ben was surprised enough to show it. He unfolded his arms and sat up straight in his seat. "No. He often spoke of Monkscombe, the countryside, its history, its customs...but never explained exactly why he had left it." He paused. "I should be interested to know."

Mr. Ferrar looked pleased. "I am at liberty to tell you, as all the persons concerned are now dead, except one—and I trust she would forgive me."

Ben raised his eyebrows.

"Two brothers," began the lawyer, settling down comfortably to his tale. "One, the elder and the heir, a sober, reliable, even-tempered boy: Harriet's father. The other, as unlike his brother as chalk is to cheese. Wild, always into scrapes and quick-tempered—although equally quick to forgive. Not a bad lad, but thoughtless and caused his family much heartbreak. He got into bad company, and took to running round with the Pardys of the day. It's a strange thing how one family, I speak of the Pardys, can cause trouble generation after generation. Strange, too, how it has always seemed to please them to embroil a Stanton in their mischief if they could."

Ben stirred uneasily, looked about to speak, and then thought better of it.

"We had all begun to wonder what would become of the boy," Jonas continued. "I'm speaking of your late father now. You are acquainted with the Misses Drew, of course?" It was a rhetorical question, for Jonas knew that Ben had met them. "Mary Drew. To see her now, a faded little mouse of a creature, you would not credit it, but she was an extremely pretty girl. Very timid and nervous, influenced by her elder sister and living in dread of her papa's displeasure, but a very sweet girl. She was good, if you understand me. She never had an unkind thought in her head. I think that was probably what took your father's fancy. On the face of it she was an unlikely girl to catch his eye, but catch it she did. I believe, had no one interfered, that she would have been a good influence on him.

"But the old rector didn't like it at all. He went to your grandfather and complained. Your grandfather liked it even less, hauled your father on to the carpet and told him in no uncertain terms that he would not allow him to ruin the reputation of a defenceless girl like Mary Drew. The rector forbade Mary to see the boy again, and poor Mary, obedient to the last, told your late father that they could not meet again. The boy felt betrayed, flew into a great rage, and swore he would leave and never come back. So he did. We heard later that he had gone to America.

"I believe," said Mr. Ferrar carefully, aware that his companion was listening closely, "that for two or three years, Mary thought he would come back for her. He didn't, of course. Whether he had actually made her any such promise, I don't know. He may have had the intention, but intentions, when one has put a few miles behind one, begin to appear differently. Your grandfather would never have his younger son's name mentioned in his presence from that time on. His other son, Harriet's father, also felt his brother had behaved badly. He thereafter felt an obligation to look after the Drew sisters, in some way which would not hurt their pride, and that is why they have always paid no more than a peppercorn rent for that nice little house."

"You said nothing of all this when I spoke of increasing their rent," Ben pointed out, breaking his silence.

"My dear fellow, I assumed that once you had met the Drew ladies you would decide, of your own free will, to leave the rent as it was."

"You didn't know me," Ben said drily. "You presumed me good-natured."

"Why not?" asked Mr. Ferrar calmly. "I knew your late father. He was a wild fellow, but without malice. Why should you not be the same? If you had insisted, despite that, on increasing the rent, then I should have told you what I am telling you now."

"And just why are you telling me now, Jonas?" Ben asked quietly.

"Because," said the lawyer firmly, "it is an easy matter to sail away from one's responsibilities. A thousand miles away, one can console oneself that whatever problems have been left behind, someone else will take care of them. Well, perhaps someone will. But that don't mean you ought not to be doing it yourself."

Ben jumped up in burst of anger and jabbed an accusing finger at the speaker. "Harriet has been talking to you!"

"I am fond of Harriet," said Jonas, growing agitated. "The girl is distressed, and I dislike to see it."

Ben put both hands flat on the desk-top and leaned over it, towering over the lawyer. "Now you just listen to me, Jonas! You told me to marry one of my cousins, and I did so. When I first came here, Harriet was so set on running Monkscombe as she saw fit that she could think of nothing else. She didn't think me fit to be its master, that she made quite clear. So I married her and made her mistress of Monkscombe, and she'll be that until she dies. I've done everything any of you ever asked of me, Jonas. Now let me alone and allow me to get along with my own life. Because I have things I want, too. Monkscombe isn't among them. I've done what's required of me here, and no one has a right to ask me to do any more."

"Tell me," Jonas countered, leaning back so that he could look up into the other's flushed face. "What is it that you want, Ben Stanton?"

"Why, to share my life with a woman, and not with a house!" he snapped. "I'm not about to discuss this any more, Jonas, because as far as I am concerned, it is all decided. I shall stay for a year, as I promised Harriet, and then I go back to Philadelphia. There's nothing more to be said. I'm a busy man, and I don't intend to waste any more time arguing over what's already settled. Good-day to you!"

He stormed out, the door slamming. Mr. Ferrar winced and searched for his old friend snuffbox. "That fellow must have exchanged brains with a mule," he muttered. "Nor does Harriet want the house. She wants *you*, you obstinate, awkward, single-minded colonial blockhead!"

BACK AT MONKSCOMBE once more, Harriet was prey to a dozen conflicting emotions. On the one hand she longed for Ben to return, but on the other she dreaded the day he did, because they would surely only quarrel again. She was already sorry that she had allowed herself to be bundled away in a hired carriage so meekly. She had been happy at Susan's, and Susan had wanted her to stay, if Ben had not been making such a fuss. Nor had he any right to make a fuss. He had behaved extremely badly, and had not offered a word of explanation, much less apology. The more she thought it over, the less she moped, and the more she grew cross. She had never in her life been dismissed like a servant. She had always been Miss Stanton of Monkscombe, her opinions listened to with respect, her wishes granted. She had given orders, not taken them. Her old resentment towards her cousin returned, based on the fact that he had come to them from nowhere and taken over all their lives. Returned, too, some of her old suspicion of him. There was so much she did not understand, and he would not explain.

James Murray rode over twice to dine with them. He was suffering his own frustrations, among them an inability to find any trace of the spy, Lesage, though he was still convinced that the man was in the neighbourhood.

"Someone is hiding him, ladies, and that's the fact of it. I just wish I knew who!" he went on wrathfully. "But it is no use asking any questions of the local people. They have a complete scorn for the law, even when it is a question of hunting traitors."

"You must not blame them." Harriet felt moved to defend the cottagers. "The West has a long tradition of being at odds with London. Besides, many of the villages are isolated, primitive places, whose inhabitants are accustomed to view anyone who lives more than a few miles away as a foreigner. Forgive me, Captain, but you cannot expect them to confide in a Scotsman.''

"If it were only the villagers, Mrs. Stanton, I could understand. But it is the attitude of many of those who should know better that I can't stomach! A magistrate who was not in his dotage would help," added James grimly. "I am no Jacobite, but whenever I talk with Sir Mortimer, I never fail to think how many good men lost their lives on Culloden Moor, and what a great pity it was that he got away with his. You know, don't you, that he was, in his youth, a follower of Stinking Billy?''

"James means the Duke of Cumberland," translated Caroline. "It's true; Sir Mortimer talks of the 'forty-five as though it were yesterday, and it was sixty years ago. I believe he worries less that Bonaparte may cross the Channel than that the Scots may arm themselves and all pour over Hadrian's Wall. He really is a funny old man.''

"He is not a funny old man, Caroline!" argued James, leaning across the table aggressively. "He is a difficult old man who insists on administering the law according to his own notions of it, is scarcely ever to be found sober—not that it would make much difference—and who generally makes my life a misery!''

So, then, thought Harriet, as she returned home across the fields the next morning, where is Lesage? She adjusted her basket, which had contained oddments she had been taking to needy cottagers, and frowned. If James were right, and the Frenchman were still near by, it seemed incredible that no one had seen him. Surely a stranger who could not give account of himself must appear odder the longer he lingered in the district?

She stopped, a sudden shudder running up her spine. But what of a stranger who *could* give account of himself? What of a man who arrived suddenly, but with a perfectly good reason for coming and staying? A man who took a great interest in surveying the sea from the Widow's Walk? A man who went to Bristol on unspecified business and watched the shipping? A man who had previously been travelling in French-occupied Europe, and who made no secret of his admiration for the Grand Army. What of Ben?

Her heart seemed to stop beating. It must be impossible, and Jonas had poured scorn on her early suspicions, but what if—if after all—she had been right?

Harriet walked on, so plunged in her speculations that she quite failed to notice that a small, ragged, grubby child waited for her in the shelter of a hawthorn hedge. She was almost upon him before she noticed him, and then gave a start.

"Why," she exclaimed, "it is young William, is it not?"

Billy Pardy moved out of his hiding-place and stood a few feet away, just out of reach and poised for instant flight. "I were waiting for you," he said, eyeing her balefully.

"What is the trouble, Billy?" she asked, adding earnestly, "Has anyone being ill-treating you again?"

"I told 'un," said Billy fiercely. "I told Aaron, if anyone come after me again, I'd split on 'em all. I'd tell the gen'leman, or you. Only the gen'leman ain't here, so I come looking for you, though I don't go running to womenfolk mostly."

Harriet turned over this involved speech in her mind. She did not quite understand all of it, but gathered that Billy was bent on revenge for some ill-usage. Her heart sank. "Is it Aaron who has been beating you?" She did not fancy tackling Aaron alone, but did not know when Ben would be back.

Billy shook his head. "Naw, Aaron is all right. Aaron only cusses. 'Tis Nathan as lays about him, and I tole 'un I'd go and tell if he did it again. Only the gen'leman is gone away," Billy added reproachfully, as if this was Harriet's fault. "An' I don't like dealing with wimmin."

The precocity with which he spoke was alarming. He was not a child, but a wizened man, too small and too young in years perhaps for manhood, but in mind he had never been a child. He had been brought up in squalor and steeped in sin. He knew no morality, he did not question the rights and wrongs of anything he had ever seen. Yet he had learned early to fend for himself, and seek to protect himself from the violence of which he was all too often the object. Above all, Billy was a Pardy. He had firm ideas on the role of women. They were to be kept in their place. One did not discuss business with them. Harriet was to understand that he was making an exception.

She sat down on the step at the foot of the stile and put her basket on the ground. Billy was as badly dressed as before, in a man's jacket much too big for his thin frame and secured around the middle with string. He was barefoot, despite the inclement weather, and did not seem to mind standing on the frozen turf.

"What is it you want to tell us, Billy? I'll see that Mr. Stanton knows of it the moment he returns."

Billy suddenly looked cunning. "'Tisn't a what, 'tis a who."

Harriet frowned. "What do you mean?"

"'Tis a fellow, what's hid down home. The Frenchie."

Harriet caught her breath. She leaned forward and asked, hardly daring to speak, "The Frenchman, Billy? Are you sure? Is this the truth?"

Billy nodded vigorously. "Nathan and Aaron went out in the boat, wi' Jethro and all, to fetch the baccy and the brandy, and they fetched back the Frenchie, too."

Harriet reflected briefly that the Pardys had a liking for biblical names, though if asked about the persons after whom they were named, they would have professed total ignorance. A little doubtfully, she asked, "And he is still there? This must have happened some time ago."

"Bust his leg," explained Billy. "Excisemen and soldiers come after 'em. They give 'un the slip, but the Frenchie bust his leg and has been laid up, down home. 'Tis mended now, and he walks with a stick, lame-like. He says he'll be off in a day or two."

So that was the explanation of it all. Lesage had been injured. Without professional care, the broken leg had been slow to heal and he was only just now able to hobble about. The Pardys, having landed the spy, were obliged to shelter him. It must be an arrangement that suited neither party, and Lesage was understandably anxious to leave as soon as he could.

What should I do? Harriet thought feverishly. Tell James Murray, was the obvious answer. But James had left that morning for a visit to Bath and would be gone some days, he had told them last night. By then,

Lesage might be gone. Sir Mortimer? He was deaf and vague, and often none too sober, but he was a magistrate. However, before she set the countryside alight, hunting for Lesage, she had to be sure that Billy was not making mischief. He was obviously athirst for revenge, and he might be making it all up to cause trouble for his family. It could be only partly true. Lesage could have been there, but already left. She could not trust Billy entirely.

"Now, listen to me, Billy," she said carefully. "It is important that you don't lie. You say you are sure of this, but I must be certain before I do anything. Now, I'll come with you down to your home, and hide nearby, and you go indoors and somehow persuade the Frenchman to come outside so that I may see him. Do you understand? He does go outside occasionally?"

"For the privy," Billy said simply. "Now his leg is mended. Before that, he..."

"Yes, yes!" interrupted Harriet hastily, not anxious to know this detail. "We'll go now, Billy."

Billy turned and set off at a trot. Harriet followed him. It was easy to conceal herself near to the Pardy cottages, for it was a wild, windswept spot. She crouched behind some bushes, shivering in the wind blowing off the sea and listening to the desolate sound of the waves breaking on the shore, as Billy made his way down the path to the door of his ramshackle home. If he was telling the truth, and Lesage were captured as a result of this, the child would have to be taken away to some place of safety before his family's wrath fell on him. But they could cross that bridge when they came to it.

Billy had gone inside, and Harriet waited impatiently. So concerned was she not to be seen from the cottage, and so intent on watching, that she had quite forgotten that she herself could clearly be seen by anyone else approaching the cottages from the track to the rear. She was abruptly and frighteningly reminded of this by the scrape of a boot. She gasped and whirled round, but too late. A pair of strong arms seized her fast round the waist, and Aaron's voice said, "Well, 'tis Mrs. Stanton! Come to visit, is it? And what are you prying into now, eh?"

"Let me go, Aaron!" she ordered in vain, twisting in his brawny grasp. "I'm not prying!"

This was so patently untrue that Aaron chuckled. "Oh, then it's come to see *me*, is it? I'm not surprised, for all you was always so proud and against me, I thought maybe you didn't mean all you said."

"You are impudent!" she snapped, angry, despite her fear.

"You've got spirit," said Aaron approvingly. "'Tis what I like about you. Generally I'm for women knowing their place and speaking when they're spoke to, but I makes an exception for you, as I always did fancy you, as you well knows."

"And I have always thought you a rogue and a ruffian, Aaron!" Harriet stormed at him. "But you are worse than I believed you, for now I know you are a traitor, too!"

The laughter left Aaron's dark eyes. "So, that's it, is it? Well, then, my dear, you'd best come on down to the house!"

He gripped her arm in an ungentle clasp and hauled her along the path to the door of the cottage. He kicked it open with a crash and sent her sprawling through, following her and slamming the door behind them.

When Harriet had regained her balance and her presence of mind, she saw that they were in a large kitchen. There was an open hearth, over which a metal stewpot hung from a hook, and a roughly made set of table and benches. Smoke from the hearth filled the room, making her cough and her eyes water, before it escaped through a broken window, in lieu of a proper chimney. Lucy Pardy, Billy's mother, a fat slattern with lank, greasy hair, stood before the stewpot and stirred it. She looked up with blank, vacant eyes. Of Billy there was no sign.

"You just sit down there," ordered Aaron, pushing Harriet down on to a bench. "Lucy, you keep an eye on her, and don't you let her slip out, or it will be the worse for you, you mark me!"

He went into a further room, and voices could be heard. Then Aaron returned, followed by a very tall man, who limped awkwardly, leaning on a stick.

"Monsieur Lesage..." whispered Harriet. "So you are here!"

He was nothing like Ben. He was tall, and the age was about the same, but in no other way did he resemble her husband. Despite her danger and her fear, she felt a surge of relief, and her heart rose. It had been nothing but her fancy, after all. How stupid she had been, and how bitterly she now regretted it!

Lesage limped over to the table, bowed and took a seat opposite her. "Mrs. Stanton? I am sorry to see you here. You realise, of course, that now you have seen me, you cannot be allowed to leave?'

Aaron had gone to the cottage door and leaned against it with his arms folded, watching.

Harriet said boldly, "I shall be missed. They will look for me."

"But not here, I fancy, *chère* madame." Lesage leaned forward and lowered his voice, so that they should not be overheard. "Mrs. Stanton, I am sorry to see you, for two reasons. One is that you are a beautiful woman, and I should be sorry to see you harmed. The other, and more important, is that your husband is an American citizen. France has excellent relations with the United States, and would not want an unpleasant incident to sour them. If something should befall you, your husband would no doubt complain bitterly to his own government. I think he is not the sort of man who would accept insult or injury and do nothing about it."

"No," Harriet agreed with an assurance she only partly felt, "he wouldn't. He would make the most terrible commotion. I know you cannot harm me." She suspected that this last statement might not be quite correct, although she was sure of the first, and Lesage's next words showed that her doubts were well founded.

"Alas, I think, Mrs. Stanton, that perhaps you do not fully appreciate your danger. For these people, this is a hanging matter. I think they will want to take you out at night in that boat of theirs, and simply push you over the side."

"'Tis a lie!" said Aaron vehemently from the door. He left his post and came to stand by the table, shoulders hunched, and his attitude threatening. "And I ain't deaf, like old Sir Mortimer, so it ain't no use a-whispering! I hears you. I don't let no harm come to the lady."

Lesage pulled a wry expression at Harriet. "You have an admirer. Unfortunately I don't believe you can have much confidence in his chivalry. He is but one. His family will think differently."

Before Aaron could reply, the door to the cottage burst open with a tremendous clatter, and the shambling form of Nathan Pardy filled the frame. He stopped and pointed at Harriet, demanding hoarsely, "What's she doing here?"

"Spying around," offered Lucy, from the hearth. She thrust back a hank of greasy hair and wiped sweat from her brow.

Aaron turned on her. "You hold your tongue! Or I'll quieten you, see if I don't!" He turned back, seized Harriet's arm and hauled her to her feet. "You wait in here." He pulled her across the room, through a door on the further side and into another room. The door slammed.

Harriet looked about her. She was in a sort of bedroom, the bed being the only piece of furniture. It was very gloomy, as there was no proper window, only a hole high up under the rafters where two or three of the stones of the cottage wall had been knocked out to let in light and air. Suddenly weak at the knees, she sat down on the bed, trying not to notice how dirty the sheets were or to think how many lice and bugs no doubt rested in the mattress. Through the door, she could hear voices. Another man had arrived, possibly Jethro. A furious argument was taking place. She could not hear everything, only odd phrases and words, but it was enough. Nathan and Jethro were for disposing of her immediately. Lesage and Aaron were against. When the other Pardy men came home, they would have the casting votes. She did not doubt which way the decision would go.

Looking round frantically for a means of escape, she climbed on the bed and peered out of the hole under the rafters. It looked much too small to allow her to wriggle through, but she could try. On the other side was a pigsty, and its odours rose to fill the room and add to the smell already there. But the grunting and scraping of its inhabitants might cover any sound she made. But if she tried now, she would be seen as she tried to run across the open ground outside. She had to wait till dusk.

She sat down on the bed again, and thought of Ben and how he would react when he arrived home to find her vanished. Lesage had been wrong to say that no one would search here for her. This would be the first place Ben would come. Instinct would lead him unerringly to Aaron. Panic filled her, this time not for herself, but for her husband. They would kill him also. They could not risk the discovery of Lesage. "Dear Ben," she thought desperately, "I wronged you so badly. How I wish..." But it was no use wishing.

A silence had fallen on the other side of the door. Cautiously Harriet went to it and tried the handle, but it was securely wedged and refused to give under her hand. She retreated back to the bed, with nothing to do but wait. After what seemed a long time, she heard a footstep on the other side of the door. Someone was coming. To fetch her away and take her bound and gagged out in the boat, to be tossed into the cold dark waters, and lost for ever? There was a scraping noise as the door was unbarred, and it swung open to reveal Aaron, alone.

Harriet jumped up from the bed and tried to face him without showing her fear. "Well, and are you decided just when you are going to dispose of me?"

He nodded, and her heart almost stopped beating, because she thought at first that he was replying to her question in the affirmative. But then it transpired that he was merely nodding to confirm an idea he had previously expressed.

"You're not afeared to speak up. But maybe, even so, you are a little afeared of me?" He grinned at her mockingly.

Harriet swallowed with difficulty, tilted her chin and said defiantly, "No, Aaron, I am not. I know you too well. You are Aaron Pardy, a ne'er-do-well, and a smuggler, if the tales told of you are true. My father was a Justice of the Peace and members of your family appeared before him more than once!"

Aaron's dark eyes narrowed. "Ay, they did, true enough. He was a powerful hard man, and I mind him well."

Harriet stared at Aaron's slovenly but handsome figure, as he slouched against the doorjamb. Was that, then, the reason for his interest in her? Did Aaron pursue some revenge against her family? "It's because of that?" she whispered incredulously.

Aaron frowned as if he did not take her meaning, then chuckled and said, "Think I worry about that? Not I. A man who gets taken up before the justices is a fool. No one did ever catch me red-handed. I be a deal too smart, do you see?" He winked at her in his familiar fashion. "But I see you do be a little afraid o' me. 'Tis no harm in that. Does add to the sport, and women do like to be mastered. They kicks and squeals, but likes it." He began to come slowly towards her, and though he smiled, something in his face frightened her more than anything so far.

"You would not dare!" she whispered.

"It be a fair bargain," said Aaron reproachfully. "You pay no attention to what the Frenchman told you. I said to you, once, that one day you'd have need of me, remember? Ah, I see you does. Well, you needs me now. I won't let them drown you. I got better uses for a pretty woman than using her for fishbait! Why don't you show me how grateful you can be?" He reached out one grimy hand and began to toy with the muslin fichu knotted on her bosom.

"You forget," she said fiercely, "that I have a husband!"

This seemed to amuse Aaron. "And where is he? Gone Bristol way, I hear, and no one knows when he's coming back. Anyway, he's a foreigner. You and I, now, is born and bred round here, almost kin."

She struck away his hand, which still fingered the fichu. "You are impudent! As if I would agree!"

"'Tis better than feeding the fishes," he pointed out. "And a pleasurable business, besides."

"No, it wouldn't be! I'd rather be dead, fed to the fish!"

"We needn't stay around these parts," said Aaron. "Go down Devon way, maybe, where no one knows us. You and I, we'd do famously together."

To her horror, she realised he was quite serious, and gasped, "You must be mad to think I would run away with you!"

"Why don't you try me, before you refuses?" he asked softly. "Change your mind, likely."

Without warning he lunged forward and pushed her sprawling back on the bed, throwing himself down on top of her. Harriet fought desperately to push him away, but in vain. She was half crushed by his weight, scarcely able to breathe, and thought she must faint or be sick, or both. Her head swam, and stars danced in and out of the blackness. She could feel Aaron's breath on her face, and hear his voice whispering obscene invitations into her ear as his hands tore at her clothing.

When it seemed that nothing could save her, help came. Aaron was jerked backwards. Harriet, sobbing, dragged herself upright, and saw that Lesage had entered and stood brandishing his stick.

"You leave the lady alone, do you hear? France wants no trouble with the United States!"

"It's nothing to me what France wants!" snarled Aaron. "I knows well enough what I wants, and that's enough!"

"Then you are wrong, my friend," Lesage said mildy, but with lurking menace. "As long as I am here, no one touches Mrs. Stanton, and especially not you. After I have gone..." He broke off and turned to Harriet with an apologetic gesture. "I am sorry, madame, but once I have left here, I cannot protect you." He turned back to Aaron. "When I have gone, you will no doubt do as you wish. But, until then, no one comes near the lady!"

He was granting her time, a stay of execution, perhaps literally, and time was what she needed. The two men went out and the door was rebarred. Harriet scrambled off the bed and tried to tidy her dishevelled clothing. She looked round frantically. She had to escape, tonight, before they remembered that hole up under the rafters.

But they had not forgotten it. A little later she heard a sound outside. The pigs squealed as someone invaded their pen. Abruptly the dim light in the room was extinguished as a board was placed over the hole from outside. The sound of hammering indicated that it was being securely fastened.

She was not to be allowed to escape. Lesage would protect her, but only for a little time. After that she would have no protection but that of Aaron, and for that he asked a price. A price she could not pay.

CHAPTER NINE

AT FIRST Harriet thought they meant to leave her in total darkness like an unfortunate lunatic in the middle ages, a twist of cruelty that might appeal to Nathan especially, and which Aaron also might employ to break her resolve. To her relief, this proved to be not so, and after a while a stub of tallow candle was brought in by a frightened child, who put it down and scurried away before Harriet could speak.

The candleflame flickered erratically and dispelled only a little of the gloom. On the other side of the door, the Pardy clan had assembled. They seemed to eat together, and they made a considerable amount of noise. She was not forgotten, and food was brought to her by another of the Pardy girls, whom she identified as Cherry. The food did not look very appetising, and was rendered less so by Cherry's putting it down and then wiping her nose on her petticoat. From the way her gown was stretched over her distended stomach, her awkward movements and the way she straightened up with a sigh and placed her hand in the small of her back, it was obvious that at almost any moment another Pardy was due to make its appearance in the world. It would be born here, without midwife or doctor, and somehow or other baby and Cherry would survive. In well-appointed homes and decent families women took the childbed fever and babies arrived stillborn. But here, in this filth, by some quirk of nature, life thrived.

Harriet wondered briefly who the father was—if Cherry knew it herself—and supposed it was one of the Pardy men, since the Pardys, like some imperial dynasties, liked to form alliances among the members of their extended family. They did so without benefit of clergy, or fidelity, changing and exchanging partners. They also did so in total defiance of the Table of Kindred and Affinity in a way that would have earned the grudging admiration of the Caesars.

Harriet picked up the spoon and stirred the stew, glad that the light was too poor to be able to see it properly. But when she tasted it cautiously it proved to be quite palatable and was composed, she fancied, mostly of rabbit and potato, with plenty of onions. There were one or two other bits floating about in it that she could not identify so readily, and these she carefully pushed to one side. She wondered if Lesage ate outside in the other room with the family, and supposed that he did. She tried to imagine, a litte amused despite her circumstances, what he made of it all. He represented something of an enigma. He could not be called a friend, but he was concerned to protect her for as long as he could.

Harriet felt a spasm of sympathy for the man. He had lain here immobilised for many weeks, probably in this room. He must have been in considerable pain from his broken leg, unable to seek proper help or nursing, suffering the slatternly ministrations of Lucy and Cherry, fearful of discovery and unable to carry out the task for which he had been sent. Things had gone badly for Lesage from the very beginning. His mission was a failure, through no fault of his own. He was unlikely to be in communication with Paris and must be unsure what to do next. Was there some way she could turn this to her advantage?

She put down the bowl of stew, unfinished. The most important question of all was, of course, where was Ben? Still in Bristol? Would he return in time to do anything to save her? If he did return, and he tried, would he be successful? And if Ben did try, what would Lesage do, anxious as he was to avoid offending the United States but depending so heavily on the Pardys?

Outside the door, the Pardys seemed in good fettle. She guessed they were drinking, and eyed the door handle a little apprehensively. Someone was singing loudly and untunefully a bawdy ballad. Once, in an interval, she heard a child crying. She wondered if it was Billy, but thought it sounded more like one of the others. So far, no one seemed to have connected her arrival with Billy, and she hoped no one did so. The room was cold and dank. Harriet huddled on the pillows, hugging her arms round herself, and settled down for a long wait.

THE FOLLOWING MORNING dawned miserably, although Harriet could not see it. Ben was only too aware of it as he rode back towards Monkscombe on the lonely and deserted road. He had set out early from Bristol and at first made good time, but now the road was potholed and rutted, it was raining—which gradually turned the surface into sticky mud—the wind cut like a knife and the landscape was dull, grey and inhospitable. He wrapped his riding-cape around him, jammed his hat down over his ears and whistled encouragingly to the horse, which was taking a poor view of all this, and plodded along, ears drooping. He shook the reins and urged it to a trot, but after a while, and several stumbles, allowed it to fall back into its pedestrian pace. At this rate he would be lucky to reach the house much before nightfall.

About half an hour and much misery later, he came to a wayside tavern of poor appearance which managed, in these circumstances, to look like a palace. He turned into its yard, slid stiffly from the wet saddle, handed over the horse to an ostler who emerged unwillingly from the warmth of the tack-room, and went into the inn.

It was a great deal better inside than out. Warm air struck his face, and a fire burning brightly offered cheery welcome. He sat down near to it, after divesting himself of his soaked outer clothing, and ordered dinner. Forgetting for a moment that he was in a country partly blockaded by the French and at war with that country, he ordered a brandy to thaw out his bones. The landlord looked furtive, muttered, "Right, sir..." and slipped away in a highly suspicious manner. A little later the brandy arrived, slipped into his hand in an equally furtive manner, accompanied by a conspiratorial wink. Probably, thought Ben wryly, the Pardys kept this place supplied as well as the rest of the surrounding countryside. For a moment he almost felt grateful to them, and began to understand the temptation for Sir Mortimer and others to regard their smuggling activities with an indulgent eye. If the money paid for this brandy ultimately bought a French musket, it did not, just at this moment, really seem so important.

Warmed by the brandy, anticipating the dinner, and toasted by the flames, he began to doze. He was awoken unceremoniously by the sudden appearance of mine host at his elbow, who hissed, "'Tis the soldiers!", seized the brandy glass out of his hand and vanished with it. The door of the tavern opened, and one red coat only appeared. Its owner's face, once he had taken off his dripping hat and shaken it, was familiar.

Surprised, but pleased at the unexpected arrival of a friend, Ben raised his arm, and called, "James! Over here!"

Captain Murray had been looking about the room. Catching sight of Ben, an expression of tremendous relief crossed his face, which seemed uncalled-for. Ben's good humour evaporated, and an instinct for trouble told him he was about to hear bad news.

James hastened across the room, shook his head energetically, and burst out, "Thank God you've come! I rode out on this road, hoping to encounter you. The weather's so foul that I thought you might have turned in here."

"What has happened?" Ben demanded sharply.

James took a seat on the oak settle beside him and lowered his voice to an urgent undertone. "A man has to believe in Providence! I should be in Bath, you know. I set out yesterday morning, but my horse went lame and I was forced to turn back. I thank the good Lord for it. Mrs. Stanton is missing, and we have not been able to find her."

Ben forced himself to speak calmly. "Since when?"

"Since quite early yesterday morning. She went out visiting the sick. She was afoot, and meaning to cut across the fields."

Ben muttered a suppressed oath. "She knows I dislike her doing that!"

"We've established that she made the visits she intended," James went on hurriedly. "She must have been on her way back. She reached a place where there's a stile, and there for some reason she must have stopped, or met someone. Her basket was found there, on the ground. But she seems to have vanished, as if she had been snatched up into the sky. We've searched in thickets and ditches in case she met with some accident, but there's not a trace. Caroline is half demented. We've every able-bodied man out looking, but so far haven't found a trace of her. Caroline is desperate for you to return, and sent me off on the Bristol road, either to meet you, or, if you weren't to be found, to ride on to Bristol if necessary and bring you back. I'm extremely glad to have found you. We can be back the sooner, and Caroline will be much encouraged."

Ben shouted to the landlord to cancel the dinner and have the horse resaddled. "You'll come with me, James? I've an idea of my own about this. I'll tell you about it as we go along." He began to struggle back into his outer clothing. "Confound it," he muttered, "I should not have left her behind, in the first place, and I should not have sent her back from Bristol, in the second. I am a dull-witted, obstinate idiot, James. You'll remember that I've told you so, and in future you'll be so good as to remind me of it!"

They took to the road again at a hazardous pace. Above the noise of clattering hoofs and the whistle of the wind, Ben yelled across to James galloping alongside him, "Have you been down to the Pardy cottages?"

"What for?" shouted James, clinging to his hat with one hand.

"Because that's where Harriet is, I'd wager everything I have on it! Don't ask me to explain now, James, it would take too long. But if you want to catch your smugglers, set a watch on the Pardys!"

The horses plunged on over difficult terrain and rendered any reply impossible. When he was again able to shout into the wind, James bawled, "What has that to do with Mrs. Stanton?"

"She must have stumbled across something, and was either lured down there or taken down there. But there she is, I know it!"

"Then we'll set her free in no time," declared James with fervour. "I'll take a troop..."

Ben was signalling disagreement, waving one hand rapidly in a negative gesture. "Bad idea! A troop of militia would be spotted a quarter of a mile away, even in this weather! They would want to get rid of the evidence and spirit Harriet away before you could burst in there! They might even dispose of her permanently! You must give me time to go down there alone, and try to get Harriet away from there before the militia arrives!"

"You're crazy, man!" yelled James, appalled. "You can't do it alone! At least, let me come with you!"

"No! I need you to ride first to Sir Mortimer, and tell him you may be making arrests and will need his services! He is back from Bristol, isn't he? After that, go and call out your men!"

James drew his horse to a plunging halt. Ben wheeled round in the middle of the road to face him, to see James's honest face, wet with rain, flushed with his exertions and radiating suppressed emotion.

"That daft old fool? Get him out to help catch smugglers? Impossible! It's my belief he is hand in glove with them! He's put nothing but obstacles in my path!''

"Listen," Ben told him urgently. "Sir Mortimer may tolerate smugglers, but in his lunatic fashion the old fellow is a patriot. Tell him the Pardys probably landed the French spy. That will change his mind!"

They arrived at last at a point some mile from the Pardy cottages, where a thicket of trees sheltered the road from view. Here they halted the lathered, mud-splashed horses, and both dismounted.

"You must give me at least two hours, James," Ben panted, leading his exhausted beast to the overhanging trees and tethering it. "It will take you that to reach Sir Mortimer and call out your men."

"I don't like it," James growled obstinately. "I'll do as you say, but it's against my better judgment. You're not even armed."

"Oh, don't be too sure of that," Ben told him with a grim smile. "On your way, Redcoat—this Yankee has need of you!"

James clattered away in a flurry of mud and grit.

Ben glanced up at the sky. It had stopped raining, which was to his advantage. Bad weather would keep all the Pardys inside their unattractive dwellings. He wanted, if possible, to lure them out—and one of them in particular. A curious look crossed Ben's face, which, had Aaron been able to see it, would have made him very uncomfortable indeed. He took off his mud-splattered riding-cape and draped it over the horse's quarters. Then he lodged his hat in a nearby branch. Finally he unwound his cravat, rolled it up and pushed it into his pocket. A man needed to be able to turn his head at a time like this, and not be dressed up like a tailor's dummy. Finally he stooped and felt inside the soft leather top of his right boot. The knife was there, in its carefully concealed compartment. He knew how to use it and, if necessary, he would.

Aloud, he murmured, "Now, Aaron Pardy, you'll find out what it is to reckon without Ben Stanton!"

He patted the horse's neck and set off across country on foot. He moved at a steady pace, keeping in the shelter of any bushes or trees, and very quietly. His boots made scarcely a sound on the wet turf, and anyone catching sight of him might have had the strange impression that a man's shadow, rather than a man, had passed across his vision. Ben reached the cottages, cast round for a suitable spot, and settled down, squatting on his heels, hidden, silent, utterly motionless, downwind of any guard dog, and waiting with the dedicated patience of the American Indian from whom he had learned to track and to ambush—either beast or man.

INSIDE THE COTTAGE, an event was about to take place that Ben could not have foreseen, and which was to place a crucial role in what followed.

Cherry Pardy came into Harriet's room, bringing with her a new stub of candle. Harriet had a feeling that, sooner or later, candlestubs would run out or prove too costly, and she would, after all, be left in darkness. Cherry seemed more distressed than usual, breathing heavily, her face blotched and running with perspiration. She bent forward to set down the candle, then uttered a sudden great shriek and collapsed on the bed, writhing and her swollen stomach heaving.

"Oh, goodness!" gasped Harriet. She ran to the door, which had been left open, and out into the other room.

Jethro and Aaron sat there at a table, playing dominoes. Jethro Pardy was a beetle-browed, ugly creature of low intelligence. As he probably could not count much beyond the number of fingers, Aaron seemed to be winning the game hands down, and was humming cheerfully under his breath. They both looked up as Harriet appeared unexpectedly before them.

"Cherry's baby is being born!" she cried.

"Oh, ah," said Jethro. "Is it?"

"I do win this game," said Aaron, ignoring the news completely to scrape all the dominoes into a heap. "That be four games I won in a row, Jethro. You be a blockhead, 'tis my opinion."

Harriet stared at them both aghast. "Didn't you hear me? Cherry is in labour."

"What do you expect us to do about it?" demanded Jethro, looking surly and peering at the dominoes in the way of a man who suspects he has been cheated but can't fathom how. "'Tis her business, and she knows how."

"Fetch some help!" cried Harriet.

"She's whelped alone before," said Jethro, unmoved, "and can do so again. You go help her if'n you wants."

"But I don't know anything about babies!" cried Harriet, growing agitated. Behind her Cherry was moaning lamentably, interspersed with gasps and shrieks.

Jethro gave a ribald guffaw. "Then us'll have to learn you! Aaron will teach you, won't you, Aaron?"

"Go and get some help!" shouted Harriet, fast losing her temper altogether, and stamping her foot, her fear of them quite eclipsed by her anger.

Aaron stared at her, then got to his feet. "I'll go fetch our Lucy, seeing as it isn't no sport sitting here playing dominoes wi' you, Jethro."

"Spots is near all rubbed off," muttered Jethro sullenly. "I ain't be going to sit here and listen to women yowling. I be going to take the dogs over to Sir Mortimer's deer-park and see if'n they can't run down an animal."

He slouched out and could be heard whistling to the two lurcher dogs. Shortly after, he could be seen through the window, setting off, the dogs at his heels. Aaron had gone to the back door and could be heard shouting for Lucy, who came running, and disappeared into the far room. Aaron followed much more slowly, sat down at the table again, and carefully filled and lit a clay pipe.

Harriet gave him a look of disgust and went back into the bedroom. On the bed lay a tiny new-born baby girl, still attached by the cord. She was purplish in colour, and puny, moving her frail arms and legs feebly and opening her mouth as if she would wail, but had not the strength. The baby, the sheets, Cherry's clothing, all were bloodstained and there was nothing with which to clean mother and baby. Harriet marched back into the other room and up to Aaron.

"We need some water."

"Well is out front," said Aaron.

"Then go and pull up a bucket."

"'Tis women's work," said Aaron. "Do you go tell Lucy to fetch it."

Harriet gasped, and then everything seemed to come to a boil inside her, her former fear, her humiliation, her revulsion for her surroundings. Her temper spilled over into rage. She flew at Aaron and boxed his ear so soundly that the clay pipe fell out of his mouth and shattered on the floor.

"Why, you useless great layabout! There is a poor woman in childbed, just delivered, one trying to help her, and a helpless babe new-born—and you just sit here smoking that pipe and refusing to do anything? I won't have it, do you hear? I will not have it! Get on your feet, you stupid great ox, and go and fetch it yourself!"

Aaron stared at her astonished, his mouth open.

Harriet, incensed because he did not move, darted forward and boxed his other ear. "Do you hear me, Aaron Pardy?"

"Oh, ay," said Aaron at last, rubbing his ear, "I hear you. No need to get your dander up and knock my head off'n my shoulders. I'll fetch the water. Do you wait here." He got to his feet and sauntered towards the door. Before going out, he paused and looked back over his shoulder. "You're a fine woman," he said seriously. "But you be powerful fierce when you're roused."

Outside, the yard was deserted. Those Pardys who remained at home—apart from Cherry and Lucy— were in the other of the pair of cottages. The pigs rooted noisily in the mud. They, at least, liked it. Bedraggled chickens perched on the wood pile about the mire obviously did not. Aaron walked whistling to the well and let down the bucket. He had hauled it to the surface and rested it on the well-rim, stretching out his arm to unhook it, when he felt the tip of a steel blade just behind his ear, and heard a voice that said softly,

"Turn round slowly, Pardy, and make no noise, or I'll slit your throat and think no more of it than if I slaughtered one of those pigs."

Aaron took his hand from the bucket. "Why," he exclaimed in genuine surprise. "I didn't hear you coming!"

"No more did you, Aaron, and be grateful I'm not after your scalp—though I'll have that if any harm has come to my wife. Where is she?"

Aaron turned to face Ben. "She's not harmed." He nodded towards the knife. "That be a strange weapon for a gentleman."

"I'm neither an Englishman nor a gentleman, Aaron, and you'd do well to remember it," Ben told him, gesturing him away from the well. "Move real slow and don't try any tricks."

"You wouldn't have got so close if'n Jethro hadn't taken the dogs wi' him," Aaron remarked, eyeing Ben insolently.

"That's the dogs' good fortune. I would have taken care of them, too."

This time Aaron eyed Ben more shrewdly. "You'm a useful sort of fellow," he said at last, grudgingly. "The lady is in yonder, worriting about women's business." He jerked his head towards the cottage behind him.

"Then go and fetch her out, Aaron, and quietly!"

Aaron scowled. "What made you so sure she is there?"

"Where else? Her basket was found abandoned by the stile. She obviously met with someone on the way home, and that person either persuaded or forced her to come here. Was it you?" Ben's tone sharpened.

Aaron's frown grew deeper. "Not I." He looked genuinely puzzled. Suddenly his brow cleared and he gave a low whistle. "Why, it be that brat of a kid. He did say he'd go tell if'n Nathan gave him another walloping. Little tow-rag, I'll skin him alive!"

"You'll do nothing but fetch out Harriet!" Ben said curtly.

A grin spread over Aaron's face. "And what's to stop me, when I get indoors, from raising the alarm?"

Ben sighed patiently. "Aaron, I've told you before. This is between you and me. I'm here only on account of my wife. I've been watching you, and your kinfolk. I know the nights you've brought in your contraband, and I've watched it loaded on to the ponies. I know you've had the Frenchman hidden here..." As Ben spoke, the look of stupified astonishment on Aaron's face increased. "But I've said nothing of it to anyone because I reckoned it wasn't my business. But when you seize my wife, it becomes my business, Aaron. You attack *me*! Now go and get her. Then we'll settle it, man to man, between us, you and I."

Aaron smiled. "Ay," he said softly, "Happen we will." He walked past Ben and unhooked the bucket, "On account," he explained, "as your lady be like to go for me like a she-cat, if'n I go back without the water." He walked towards the cottage, and stooping beneath the low lintel, went inside.

Ben moved prudently behind the well-head in case anyone in the house had any kind of gun trained on him. He had to wait for some minutes, but that was not Aaron's fault.

"About time, too!" said Harriet crossly. "Put the water down there. What took you so long? Is it the first time you ever hauled up a bucket of water?"

"You've a powerful sharp tongue!" said Aaron fervently, dropping the bucket and spilling half its contents. "And I begin to think I'll be glad to see the back of you. Lucy, do you come and fetch this water! You, Mrs. Stanton, come with me."

"I can't," said Harriet. "I'm busy."

Aaron's face turned brick red beneath the bronze, grime and whiskers. "I never in all my born days met a female so contrary. First you was for me letting you go, then you was for taking over and giving I orders. Now, dang it, you'm refusing to budge when I do want to give you back to your husband! I do begin to feel sorry for him. He be welcome to you!"

"Ben?" cried Harriet, "Oh, Aaron, is Ben here? Please tell me the truth?"

"Ay, the fellow is outside, and don't know when he be well off or he wouldn't have come looking for you. Do you go out quiet! You'll bring everyone out into the yard if you runs out shouting and squeaking!"

But Harriet had darted out of the open door and ran across the yard and into Ben's arms. She clung to him tightly, and burst into tears, of relief and joy. "Oh, Ben, oh, my darling, I knew you would come, and I wanted you to, so much, and at the same time I was so frightened they would kill you . . ."

Ben put his arm round her shaking body pressed desperately against him, and knew that, no matter what he had ever said, he would never be able to go now and leave her behind. "You win, Jonas," he thought ruefully.

Aaron had followed her out into the yard, and stood a little way away, watching them. Ben saw him, and pushed Harriet gently aside.

"I'm not finished here yet, Harriet. You start for home. I'll catch up with you shortly."

"What are you going to do?" she whispered, suddenly afraid.

Before he could answer, they were unceremoniously interrupted. Jethro appeared, running full tilt, waving his hat and shouting, "Soldiers be coming here! I met with Nathan, and he saw 'un on 'tother side of the village! Soldiers be coming!"

The response to his cry was amazing. Men, women and children tumbled out of the other cottage and began to disperse in all directions with incredible rapidity. Even the pigs ran for the shelter of their sty. There were two exceptions to the general exodus. One was Lesage, who appeared in the doorway of the second cottage, calmly loading and priming a pistol. The other was Aaron, who indeed turned to run, but was stopped by Ben, who, with a yell of "No, you don't!" threw himself full length, and wrapped his arms around Aaron's knees, bringing him plunging to the ground.

The two men rolled over and over in the mud, wrestling, punching, swearing, kicking and gouging in a vicious struggle which knew no rules. Harriet watched horrified, both hands clasped to her mouth. Eventually the combatants came to a rest, up against the pigsty, Ben sitting on Aaron's chest and his hand grasping Aaron's throat.

"Get off I!" croaked Aaron, choking, and so caked in mud that he was scarcely recognisable.

Ben, in hardly better state, struggled to his feet, hauling Aaron up with him. When both were upright, Ben drew back his fist and dealt his opponent a fearsome blow to the jaw, which sent Aaron sprawling back into the mud again.

Ben walked back towards Harriet, attempting, in vain, to improve his appearance by straightening his sleeves. Besides being covered in mud, he had a rapidly swelling black eye, and blood smeared his face from a cut lip.

"You look dreadful..." whispered Harriet.

"I feel just great!" he said with deep satisfaction.

"Then perhaps, you would stay just where you are, Mr. Stanton," said Lesage politely, limping out of the shelter of the doorway from which he had watched the fight with interest, and levelling the pistol at Ben's chest. "You and I, I hope, will settle matters without violence."

"Put that away," Ben told him wearily. "I've always known you were here. It's not my quarrel. But I've a suggestion to make, and I think you should follow it."

Lesage raised his eyebrows and gestured slightly with the pistol to indicate that Ben should continue.

"To my mind," said Ben, "you've not done anything to warrant arrest. You've done no spying. You have paid for any intention of doing so by being shut up all this time with the Pardys, a severe enough punishment for anyone. My suggestion is that you contact your smuggler friends—when you can find wherever they've disappeared to—and get them to return you to the next French ship they sail out to meet. Go back to France, monsieur. Better luck next time."

Lesage smiled, and slipped the pistol into his pocket. "Mr. Stanton, I regret we should have met in such adverse circumstances. Such is war. I regret, too, most sincerely, the unfortunate imprisonment of madame." He bowed to Harriet. "I shall not be sorry, as you can imagine, to leave the hospitality of the Pardys. The food," said Lesage, with a shudder, "defies description. And, my dear Stanton," he lowered his voice, as one about to make a confidence between men, "have you seen their women?"

A tremendous clatter caused them all to turn their heads. A carriage was bouncing over the rough terrain towards them, rattling and clattering so much that it seemed it must disintegrate. It plunged to a halt a short distance away. Aaron staggered to his feet, rubbing his jaw, and eyed it warily, as its door was flung open.

"Aaron Pardy!" screeched Sir Mortimer, with astonishing volume for an eighty-six-year-old pair of lungs. "Come over here this minute, you scoundrel!"

"So 'tis you, then, Sir Mortimer," said Aaron sullenly.

"Of course it is, confound your impudence! You wretch, I'll see you hang! Get over here and help me out of this confounded carriage! I'm half shook to death!"

Aaron made his way to the carriage with some alacrity, and helped Sir Mortimer to descend to *terra firma*, even if the ground was less firm than he might have wished. The magistrate stood, teetering insecurely, and brandishing his stick at all and sundry.

"He's been at the White Lightning again," said Ben resignedly to Harriet.

"What is it?" she asked bewildered.

"Sugarcane spirit, from which they distil the rum eventually. He has it sent from Jamaica—by the barrel, I shouldn't be surprised!"

Aaron reached into the interior of the carriage and withdrew the magistrate's hat. He gave it a brush with his sleeve, rendering it, if anything, muddier than it had been before, and set it on Sir Mortimer's aged head.

By way of recompense, Sir Mortimer struck him a not inconsiderable blow on the shoulder with his stick. "You are a dog, sir! A confounded mongrel cur—worst of a bad litter!"

"If'n you says so," said Aaron carelessly. "You're the magistrate."

"I do say so! I am the magistrate, and have been the magistrate here for seven and thirty years! I know the law, sir, and don't need a Scotsman to tell me it! Fellow came galloping up to my front door, wearing a militia uniform and hollering and creating a fuss like a madman. I saw he was a Scotsman straight off! Had the impudence to tell me my business! I told him I needed no Scotsman to tell me how to administer the law, and to mind his own business!"

"Poor James," said Harriet.

"Aaron," ordered Sir Mortimer, "give me your arm, you useless rogue. Damn layabout! I've a fancy to view the sea. Over there..." Sir Mortimer waved his stick toward the horizon and proceeded thence, wobbling unsteadily and heavily supported by Aaron.

"I've seen some strange sights," Ben observed in a low voice to Harriet, "but that just about beats all."

"You'd do best to go no further," bellowed Aaron into the magistrate's ear. "'Tis the cliff edge, and you'll likely fall over, your legs being shaky."

This time Sir Mortimer dealt him a crack over the head with his stick, and ordered, "Hold your tongue, you uncouth spawn of an unsanctified and probably illegal union! Help me to sit down, there, on that rock."

With some difficulty, he was seated, and rested his stick on the ground and surveyed them all. It ought to have been a ridiculous sight, but instead it was a curiously impressive one. Out here, in this primitive place, the scene resembled some ancient tribal council. Sir Mortimer's great age and white hair gave him, seated on his rock, the air of a village elder with his baton of office. His authority was undisputed, even by Aaron, who shifted his feet uneasily. Sir Mortimer knew his own people, and had come among them to dispense judgment. They all waited.

Raising the stick, he pointed it first at Lesage. "Who is that?"

"He came with the brandy," said Ben loudly. "And is going back the same way!"

"Fair enough," said Sir Mortimer, obviously not wishing to interfere with the free passage of the valuable spirit. "Tell him to clear off before a horde of Scots militiamen arrive."

"I shall go," said Lesage hurriedly. "I bid you all farewell." He began to make off rapidly.

"Ah, Stanton," said Sir Mortimer in a change of tone, momentarily sidetracked. "And Harriet, my dear..." He raised his hat. "Glad to see you up and about. Fully recovered?" These baffling civilities dispensed, Sir Mortimer returned his attention to Ben.

"It's a great pity we are not at my house, Stanton, and can discuss this like gentlemen. My butler this morning decanted a very fine port. But it don't travel. However, to matters in hand. Pardy!''

"I'm listening," said Aaron warily.

"Fair sailor, ain't you?''

"Reckon so," agreed Aaron with well-found caution.

"Need men for the Navy," observed Sir Mortimer artfully. "I hear the press gang is in the neighbourhood." He tapped the side of his nose. He looked both wily and malicious, like some ancient hobgoblin, apt to play tricks such as curdling the milk and making the cows dry.

"I never heard tell on it!" exclaimed Aaron, startled.

Sir Mortimer looked momentarily disconcerted. "Oh? Then it will be next week. Cap'n Lomas sent me a crate of rum and a note about it—so that I should know not to interfere, if the relatives come complaining. Aaron, you've caused over and above enough trouble in these parts. Time to serve your King, sir, and your country! Before the mast! Go and volunteer."

"I ain't one for living on salt pork," objected Aaron in a surly tone.

"You've not much choice!" retorted Sir Mortimer crisply. "Either that, or I'll personally see you are transported to Botany Bay—and you won't like that! Australia is worse than America, they tell me." He poked Aaron vigorously in the stomach with his stick. "So be on your way, before the militia arrives—and takes you off to hang."

"Oh, well," said Aaron, "Looks like I be going to see the world." He shrugged his shoulders and set off at a fast pace.

"Well, that's settled that," said Sir Mortimer genially. He began to struggle to rise, and both Ben and Harriet ran to help him.

"Shocking bad character, Pardy," confided Sir Mortimer to them, breathlessly, as he dangled between their supporting arms like a collapsed puppet. "Not surprising. Bad breeding-stock. Not a thoroughbred among 'em. But fine sailor, and a pity to waste it. Let the Navy hang him, if it wants to; no need for anyone else to do it."

Ben reflected that if Aaron stayed any length of time with the Navy, swinging from the yardarm was probably how he would finish—but that it was more likely that he would jump ship at the first suitable port.

They all proceeded to the magistrate's carriage and were borne, jolted, back to where Ben had left his horse. Here Sir Mortimer set them down, and took his leave.

"Good to see you, Stanton, You, too, Harriet, my dear, although in my young day a woman lying-in took to her bed. Now, I see, they go gallivanting about the countryside. It don't do. All these new-fangled ideas are a lot of nonsense. Stanton, take your wife home and put her to bed!"

CHAPTER TEN

IT WAS EARLY EVENING by now, and already dusk, as the winter twilight that draws in so quickly gathered over the landscape. Ben lifted Harriet up on the horse, and threw the riding-cape around her. Then he grasped the bridle and led the animal back to the road.

"If it won't trouble you," she said hesitantly, "I should like to stop at Dr. Gray's house to ask if he would go to see Cherry Pardy. She is lying in, and the poor creature has had little help or care. I'll pay the doctor his fee."

Dr. Gray, to his credit, agreed to go at this late, dark hour to such a disreputable place as the Pardy home without a single objection, and set off on his roan cob, with a boy walking ahead to light the path with a lantern. Harriet and Ben resumed their slow way home.

In the now near total darkness, with only a little fitful moonlight casting an erratic illumination on the road, it was difficult to make more of Ben than a tall, dark shape walking silently alongside the horse. A swish of wings overhead marked the passage of an owl that had quitted the rafters of a barn on its nightly prowl. Harriet, Ben and the horse moved through a new night-time world. Some creatures slept, but others were awake and about their business. Eyes watched them. Foxes, rabbits, stragglers for survival in an inhospitable winter world. The undergrowth rustled beneath the passage of invisible paws. Sharp little nails scrabbled at the frozen earth, and a frightened squeak betrayed some small creature which, unwary, had fallen prey to a swift darting swoop of the owl. Somewhere out there, too, was the dispersed Pardy tribe. Yet Harriet did not feel afraid, because she was with Ben. She even began almost to wish that they would not reach Monkscombe. That they would go on walking along like this, cocooned in darkness. Ahead of them was nothing but an unwished moment of reckoning, and at the thought of it, her heart failed.

Occasionally, when the horse jibbed at a curious hump or unfriendly shadow, Ben spoke soothingly and encouragingly to it, but to Harriet he had nothing to say. It was not a good omen.

A quarter of a mile from the house they met with another rider: loyal Joe Henderson, patiently casting back and forth on the road, seeking news. Ben sent him on ahead to tell Caroline that all was well and to expect them shortly.

Their arrival at Monkscombe was, naturally, both lively and noisy. The house was ablaze with lights, and alive with people running out to meet them and running back inside again to tell anyone who had not heard the glad news. Caroline cried and laughed and hugged her sister, and then Ben, and Harriet again, and declared she had been worried half to death, and so had James, and all the servants and everyone. Then at last Joe had come galloping up to the front of the house, shouting that Mrs. Stanton was found and was coming back with the master. Mrs. Woods the housekeeper had promptly burst into tears, and Cook, who was Irish and had been fortifying herself in the crisis with the cooking sherry, had fallen to blessing every

saint in the calendar. Caroline had run out on the
portico and waited in the cold wind in her gown and a
light shawl, and now here they were at last and she did
not know whether to laugh or cry herself, she said,
while managing successfully to do both at the same
time. Then practical needs took over, and maids were
sent scurrying up and down the stairs with pails of
bath-water, because the one thing both Ben and Harriet sorely needed was to wash away the accumulated
grime of an encounter with the Pardys.

Harriet, once she had bathed and washed her hair,
and told the servant to throw away all the clothes she
had been wearing for fear of fleas, dressed in a fresh
gown, wrapped her damp hair in a turban and went
downstairs to supper. The routine of the house was
turned topsy-turvy, but a small collation had been put
out for Mr. and Mrs. Stanton in the study, on a little
table before a roaring log fire. The little room was cosy
and welcoming. Its familiar furniture and book-
shelves, its worn old carpet and its sporting prints on
the walls were reassuring old friends.

Ben was already there, sitting in front of the fire,
staring down into it, and she remembered finding him
thus once before—it seemed an age ago, and yet it was
really a very little time. So much had happened. And
so much had happened to her. She was not the same
Harriet, and would never be that old Harriet again.
She wondered if all their experiences had wrought any
changes in Ben, or whether she had never really known
him well enough to be able to tell.

He looked up and asked, "All in order now?"

"Yes, only my hair is still wet, and I hope you don't
mind the turban."

They sat at either side of the little table, in the flickering firelight, and picked at the food. Neither seemed very hungry. At last, unable to bear the silence any longer, Harriet said, her eyes fixed on her plate,

"I dare say you are angry because I went to the Pardy house and allowed myself to be taken their prisoner. It is only because I did not know whether to believe Billy, and I didn't know when you would return. I thought James had left, too. I didn't know he would be coming back so soon."

He cut short her trail of excuses. "It's no matter, Harriet. It's all over and done with. There's little to be gained by squabbling over the details. If a thing's done and can't be altered for the better, it's best let alone. Chalk it up to experience, if you wish."

"Do you think poor James will catch any of the Pardys'?" she asked.

"I doubt it," Ben said shortly, his long fingers picking a piece of bread into a pile of crumbs, which he swept up methodically into a little pyramid. "The luckless James is, I fear, doomed to failure. He's in the wrong business. He'll be riding hell for leather all over the countryside right now, and will be lucky to hunt down any of the women or children. The menfolk will have their bolt-holes, like so many rats. When they all came piling out of that cottage, it appeared to me nothing so much as a disturbed rats' nest. A pity the terrier I meant to send among them—James Murray—arrived too late! They will all lie low for a little, until the militia gives up and goes away, then slowly drift back to their old haunts. Apart from Aaron, of course, who—if he isn't in the brig—will probably be instigating a mutiny on some British ship of the line.

A few more Jack Tars like Aaron, and the French fleet won't need to fire a shot! I doubt Sir Mortimer did the Navy any favour."

"Just so long as he never comes back..." Harriet said quietly but with deep feeling, and Ben glanced up at her averted face.

"You know, Harriet," he said after a moment's hesitation, "you ought not to blame yourself too much about that. You'd known Aaron all your life, and familiarity breeds contempt, as they say—you forgot to be afraid of him."

"I was always afraid of him, I knew he was a bad character. I forgot to be afraid of him at the end only because I was so angry to see him so unfeeling and useless—over Cherry's needs."

Ben was shaking his head. "No—you forgot to be afraid of him before that. You had become used to your fear; it had become just a part of the way you saw him. Real fear breeds an instinct to be wary, to take care. You rushed in unwarily because your fear of Aaron was already such a normal, ordinary thing that it no longer did its job. It no longer warned you. Well, we can chew this one over half the night, I dare say, and get no further forward. Let it alone, Harriet, past is past. Forget it."

She wanted to say, "I shall not forget any of it, ever", but was silent.

"I was pretty stupid, though," Ben said reflectively, and she looked up in surprise to hear this admission on his lips. "I shouldn't have left you here alone, not without settling Aaron's hash first. My mistake. It was like leaving a farm with a cougar wandering around the neighbourhood. You can't trust it not to make trouble before you get back. I'm not too good at explaining myself, Harriet. I never had to, I guess. I mean, I never had to explain my intentions or detail my plans to anyone. I always just went ahead and did what I wanted, because it didn't matter to anyone but me. It never occurred to me that you had any kind of right to know what I was about. I should have explained myself better from the start. I shouldn't have come prowling round the place unannounced. I should have told you what I'd discovered about the Pardys—their smuggling and the Frenchman. I should have told you why I went to Bristol, which was only a simple business visit involving merchant shipping offices. I wasn't preparing a report on the effectiveness of the French blockade for Bonaparte's bedtime reading.''

A gently mocking tone touched his voice. Harriet turned crimson, and hoped that in the firelight he could not notice it.

In an altered voice, he added abruptly, ''And I'm sorry you saw me with the girl. It was only the one time.''

''You don't need to explain that to me,'' Harriet said quietly.

''Sure I do. I'm just sorry about it. I was sorry about it long before I saw you and found you knew about it. It was just—just one of those things. Well, I can't explain that to you, Harriet. Men are made that way, I guess.''

She mumbled, ''Yes, I suppose so.'' She wanted to ask, ''Then what about me? Don't I inspire the same reactions? The same instincts? Am I, Harriet Stanton, just so untouchable, like a cold marble statue, that you never feel the same way about me?'' She had even opened her mouth to ask this, prompted by desperation, but at that moment they were interrupted.

A stamp of feet outside the door heralded the appearance of James Murray, looking much saddle-worn and out of temper.

"I came to see you were all right, Mrs. Stanton. You, too, Ben..." He peered into the firelit gloom. "Man, you've been in a bonnie fight!" said James with respect. "I'd surely like to have seen it."

"It was a real good fight," said Ben appreciatively—and Harriet thought that really she would never understand men!

"Two women and five children," said James with a return to his former gloom. "What a bag for tonight's hunt! The men have vanished. I let the women go. No point in hauling them off to Bridewell. Both the women seemed simpletons, or knew how to act poor wee dafties for my benefit, I don't know which—and frankly, I don't care!" James threw himself down in a chair, and accepted the glass of wine Ben poured for him.

"You'll stay the night, James?" Ben asked.

The Captain shook his head. "Thank'ee, I can't. I've a troop of men outside. Caroline ordered that they all be given mulled ale, and if I don't round them up soon and get them back to barracks, they will all disappear like the Pardys! You know," he said seriously, "I really think this is not my calling."

"Oh, poor dear James," said Harriet commiseratingly, when he had departed. "Whatever's to be done about him and Caroline?"

"He's too conscientious. I'm too tired to discuss his troubles tonight and, I'm pretty certain, so are you."

Ben got to his feet. "Away to your bed, lassie, as James would say—tomorrow is another day."

HE MIGHT BE TIRED, but Ben could not sleep. He tossed on his pillows, and turned over his conversation with Harriet. It was all very well to tell the girl to chalk up her mistakes to experience, but what of himself? To what should he attribute his mistakes, and, more to the point, what could he do about them? "Not much," he muttered to himself. As he had told Harriet, you can't go altering the past to eliminate your errors. You could, however, learn from them. There was no shame in that. The shame lay in not doing so.

Ben twisted in the sheets, propped his head on his folded arm, and because thinking along those lines got him nowhere, began to think about James and Caroline. Harriet had asked him what they could do to help the couple. Turning the problem over and over in his mind, he suddenly found himself meditating a solution. It was a pretty good solution, and seemed so simple and obvious, that for a moment enthusiasm fired his soul and he sat up in bed in the darkness, resting his arms on his knees and frowning as he worked out all the details. Then he reflected that it wouldn't do, because it involved Harriet and required her to make a decision she would be loath to make, and which he could not ask her to make. It required her to make a whole string of decisions.

All the same, he could suggest it to her. No, it would be a waste of time. Ben argued with himself in this way for some time, until he had worked himself up into such a pitch of wakefulness that he could stay in bed no longer and climbed out. The room was cold, and it

took him some minutes to light a candle which flickered unevenly in the draught. The house was full of
such draughts. The wind entered through ancient
cracks and crannies and, on stormy nights, whistled
eerily in the roof timbers. It was not the climate for
sitting about in a nightshirt, and he half dressed himself again, after a fashion, pulling on his breeches and
his stockings, and tucking in his nightshirt, before at-
tacking the dead embers of the fire with a brass poker.

It was beyond resurrection. He wondered if the
study fire was still smouldering, and went downstairs. But instead of just going into the study, he
found himself going from room to room, carrying the
candle in his left hand, and picking up and examining
all manner of odd objects. Caroline's music. Harriet's needlework, abandoned in the morning-room. He
remembered Harriet sitting here, sewing on lace for
Caroline—why couldn't Caro sew on her own lace?—
when he had come in with his proposal of marriage.

No, Ben corrected himself firmly. When he had
come in with *Jonas's* proposal of marriage. What a
prize gudgeon he must have looked and sounded!
What an incredibly pompous bore! Why had the girl
not just laughed in his face? That would have served
him right and taught him a lesson.

"And why," asked Ben, setting down his candlestick and turning the little piece of embroidery he had
found this way and that, "did she agree?"

She had agreed because she had not had the self-
confidence to refuse him. She felt herself obliged to
provide for Caroline, to ensure the smooth running of
the house, to heed the advice of an old and valued
friend. What she had not had the courage to do was to
heed her instincts and shout No! Later on, of course,

she had tried to back out, but in such a ladylike way that it had annoyed him. He had refused to accept her attempt at polite and tactful breaking of the engagement simply because he had wanted, obscurely, to force her to speak openly. To stand up and shout out what she really felt. But the only time Harriet felt confident enough to shout was when it was some matter affecting Monkscombe. In the same way, she had been afraid of Aaron until it was a question of standing up for Cherry's needs. Always other people, but never herself. She carried self-sacrifice and duty to a fault.

He threw himself down on the nearest chair and fiddled with the embroidery as these thoughts ran through his head. Absent-mindedly, he pulled out the needle and began to push it back and forth until he realised, to his horror, that he had succeeded in making several large and ugly stitches all over her work and the silks had knotted themselves mysteriously into a Gordian knot which would have baffled Alexander. "That's all I need," he thought. "Now I have to explain to Harriet why I came downstairs in the middle of the night and sabotaged her embroidery. I'll be lucky if she doesn't send for Dr. Gray!" He dropped the scrap of material and, like a guilty child, turned it over, so that the damage could not be seen at first glance.

He picked up the candlestick, the stub now guttering dangerously low, and made his way back upstairs. It took him past Harriet's door. He paused there, wondered if she was asleep, wished he could go in and tell her his idea about James and Caroline, wished . . . He scowled, hunched his shoulders and continued on his way. At the turn of the corridor he paused, glanced back, and turned back, retracing his steps. The only time they had shared a room had been two uncomfortable nights at Lady Williams's house, and he had spent those in a chair. Ben wondered vaguely if there was any history of insanity in the family, and he had inherited it. Harriet in her nightgown, with her long brown hair curling on her shoulders, had been an altogether pleasing and delightful sight. He reached out his fingers and touched the door-knob, then let them slide away again. Harriet...

HARRIET WAS DREAMING. It was a disturbing and frightening dream, in which she was running over the moor with the fleeing Pardys. Aaron held her fast by the hand and dragged her along. Behind them pounded the hoofs of the horses of James Murray's troopers, and somewhere in the far distance was Ben, whom she wanted to reach and could not. She awoke, sweating and with her heart beating painfully. For a moment, in the darkness, she almost believed herself back in the Pardy cottage. But putting out her hand, and encountering the lace edging of the pillow, she knew she was home again at Monkscombe. Home again, and alone again in her bed.

She sat up and sighed. Her heart no longer beat in terror, but there was a lingering ache in it that would not go away. It would always be so, unless she could find some way to tell him that she loved him. Perhaps there was a way. Desperate situations call forth desperate measures. Ben, it seemed, would never come to her bed. But she could go to his. The worst that could happen would be for him to send her away, but, even then, she would be no more badly off than now.

Harriet slid out of the sheets and felt with her fingers for her night-rail. It must have fallen on the floor, because she could not find it. It was chilly outside in the corridor, but she would have to brave it in her nightgown. She crept to the door and, opening it, stepped out. The last thing she expected was to find someone standing outside it, and she gave a cry of terror. The yellow flickering light of the candle blinded her for an instant, and she could not make out who it was. For a dreadful moment, she thought Aaron had come for her.

"It's only I, Harriet!" Ben said quickly, realising that she could not quite make him out. "Don't be scared."

She could see him now, peering down at her in concern. He was wandering about in his stockinged feet for no apparent reason, and she stammered, "What are you doing?"

"To tell you the truth," Ben said. He stopped, and there was a long pause. "To tell you the truth," he said, suddenly and all in a rush, "I was about to open your door."

Harriet stared at him, wondering if this was really happening or merely another part of another dream. "Really?" she faltered.

"Yes, really." He sounded faintly obstinate, and was too obstinate, still, to say that he wanted her so much that he no longer cared about any arguments for or against. Instead, he muttered, "I had an idea about James and Caro, and I thought... But what are you doing?"

"Well, I..." Harriet gulped. "I... Oh, Ben, I was doing the same thing, coming to find you."

He said, "Oh, darnation, Harriet..." and set down the guttering candle and put his arms round her.

Harriet pressed her face into his chest, and mumbled, "I love you. I don't know how to say it in any other way."

"There isn't any other way," he whispered into her hair. "Harriet, forgive me. I'm a stupid and obstinate idiot. Give me a choice of decisions, and I'll make the wrong one. Harriet, I missed you so much when I was in Bristol. I wanted you there with me. But when you came, I sent you away again, and hated myself for it, and wanted you back...and just—just messed everything up pretty thoroughly, I guess."

She sniffed into the front of his shirt, and he begged her anxiously, "Don't cry!"

"I'm not crying, I'm happy!" said a defiant, muffled voice.

Ben said, "Come on," and put his arm round her shoulders, collected the light and led her back into the bedroom. As he pushed the door shut, the candle stub gave a last despairing flicker and expired. He put down the holder, cupped both hands round her face, raising it towards his, and kissed her. She twisted her arms round his neck, clinging to him.

"I don't love the house more, Ben, truly. I don't want it without you in it. I want a home like Susan's with babies and lots of mess and muddle and people happy in it."

"Sure," he said huskily. "And so do I." He felt her slender body shudder beneath his touch through the cotton nightgown. "You're going to catch cold." He took his arms away from her reluctantly, and gave her a gentle push in the direction of the bed.

Harriet scrambled back in, and listened to him struggling out of his clothes in the darkness. The sheet twitched, the feather-bed subsided, and he was beside her. He put his arm round her and she rolled into his embrace in the warm nest of the pillows. She slid her hand over the damp warm skin of his chest, and whispered, "I wanted you to love me."

"I do love you—I did love you. Heck, Harriet, I loved you when I first set eyes on you! But I fought it. Oh yes, I was so mule-headed, I'd have won a prize if they handed out prizes for downright stupidity! Hey, Ben Stanton, I said to myself, you don't need her. But I do need you. I couldn't go away and leave you. I know I said I meant to, but I don't think, when the time came, that I could have done it. The trouble was, you thought me such a barbarian. That hurt at the time, but perhaps you were right."

"No, I wasn't. I was bigoted and ignorant and stupid."

"And beautiful." His mouth sought and found hers. "And I just wished," he said after a few moments, "that you had trusted not just me, but yourself enough."

"I do," she said simply. "I do now." She touched his face with her fingertips. She felt none of the shyness or awkwardness she had thought she might feel at this time. It seemed right and natural to be here with him. And it was right and natural, because he was her husband, and she loved him and knew now that he loved her. Yet in a way they were both like children, innocents in a new world that contained only themselves. A new Adam and Eve in the garden, making again that same old discovery. Their hands touched each other's bodies almost with wonder until his touch grew more impatient, and she, responding, whispered, "Love me."

He whispered, "Oh, Harriet, I never wanted anyone like I want you."

Somewhere in the house, the ancient woodwork settled down in the changing night temperatures with a groan. Perhaps the house was feeling its years. Perhaps it was glad that a Stanton who had wandered away had come back, and that matters taking the course they were, it was likely that plenty more little Stantons would hide in its attics, slide down its banisters and skate on its newly-polished parquet floors. Perhaps it realised, though it had won one battle, it had lost another. It had lost its hold on Harriet. Ben had taken his rightful place.

Some time later, Harriet, in Ben's arms and Ben's wife at last, murmured, "What did you want to tell me about Caro and James?"

"Oh, that." He settled back on the pillows, and she nestled into his shoulder. "It was a fancy I took in my head. But it doesn't matter. I'm staying here now, at Monkscombe, so it was only a notion."

Something in the way he said "staying at Monkscombe", not a note of regret, but of acceptance, told her what she had to do and say, now, immediately, or she would, one day, hear that note of regret.

"I don't want us to stay here," Harriet said. "I want us to go to America. I want you to take me to Philadelphia. If you like, we can even go and find that wild new country you told me of, where there is no one but the Indians and the buffaloes, and we can find ourselves a piece of land and build a new Monkscombe. Our own Monkscombe, yours and mine."

His arm about her tightened its grip. "You really mean that?" Eagerness touched his voice.

"Yes, I really do."

"Because I thought..." He paused, then plunged on. "I thought, if ever you...if ever I succeeded in persuading you to do that, to come back home with me, we could leave Caroline and James to run Monkscombe. James is the sort of fellow who would make a good job of it. The tenants would accept him if he were married to a Stanton. Caroline would stay here, where she's happy."

"Why, that's perfect!" Harriet exclaimed. "You are clever."

"Well, let's call it practical. Not a great hand at all the social graces, perhaps, but pretty good in other ways. Speaking of which..." said Ben, turning towards her, "I don't want to talk about Caro and James right now. Only you and me."

"Only you and me," she promised. "Now and always."

Harlequin Regency Romance™

COMING NEXT MONTH

#9 SWEET DORO by Dixie Lee McKeone

Finding herself in London for the Season is a great surprise to Lady Dorothea Sailings. Widowed for six years, she has been living in the country with her young charges, whom she has now reluctantly brought to London for a bit of town polish. But the real surprise is becoming reacquainted with Garreth Amberson, Viscount Tolver, who has also brought his ward to London for the first time. Although sixteen years have passed, Doro and Garreth agree to join forces "in the best interest of the youngsters," only to learn how little their own interest has changed.

#10 THE DEVIL'S DARE by Jean Reece

An unexpected accident brought Lord Dare to Elaine Farrington's rescue. Knowing Lord Dare to be called The Devil's Dare for his rakish ways and madcap pranks, Elaine resisted his persistent advances. Yet her brother, Nicholas, considered Dare a great gun. Consequently, Lord Dare was admitted to their home and hearth on a regular basis. In the meantime, Elaine learned that the Scottish Regalia was missing and that someone suspected it was secreted in her house. When threatening notes arrived and trespassers were detected, Elaine had to face the unpleasant truth. Who else but Lord Dare had unlimited access to her house? Who else but Lord Dare would accept a mission so devious? There was nothing for it. The man she had sworn never to love was a traitor to the English Crown.